I leaned back i
was still staring at
feel uncomfortable ɑ

"Listen, Renn," I managed to say. "About earlier."

"I should have just told you." He moved his hands from his lap to the table and started twirling his fingers again. "I'm doing a report on coffeehouses."

"I mean about what happened with the bicycle."

His body stiffened slightly. He averted my eyes as he reached for his coat. The material made a soft crinkly sound.

"Where did you go?" I asked.

"I had business to take care."

"I mean, you disappeared. You didn't just go around the corner. You…you vanished."

A ton of emotions crossed his face. Anger. Concern. Surprise. He didn't seem sure of himself. One thing I did know, he knew exactly what I was talking about.

"Tell me how?"

"Sometimes things happen that we can't explain." He placed his hand next to mine on the table, moving it so that our pinkies touched. Oh, God. Tingles ripped through me. I looked at his long, smooth fingers.

With the other hand he tapped an icon on his tablet, the muscles in his face tightening.

"Is everything okay?" I asked.

He didn't answer.

"Do you need more information for your article?"

He scrunched his eyes. A confused look passed across his face.

"For your coffeehouse piece?"

"Ah." He shook his head. "I'm good."

The Time Traveling Matchmaker

by

Janie Emaus

The Time Traveling Matchmaker

Cover Art by *Jennifer Greeff*

The Wild Rose Press, Inc.
PO Box 708
Adams Basin, NY 14410-0708
Visit us at www.thewildrosepress.com

Publishing History
First Edition, 2022
Trade Paperback ISBN 978-1-5092-4101-9
Digital ISBN 978-1-5092-4102-6

Published in the United States of America

Dedication

For my mom, who has always believed in me.

Chapter One

Once upon a time, I believed in happily ever after.
Now I only believed in after.

After summer. After film school. After breakfast. After yoga. After my break.

The line this morning at The Mud Hut stretched from the counter to the doorway. As I stood behind the bar, my mind traveled over the familiar faces. Past the "double mocha, hold the whip," over the "vanilla latte, extra hot," beyond the "tall drip of the day," and into a future where I wasn't making drink orders and wearing a forced smile.

Into a future where I was doing something important, making a difference. That place had to be out there somewhere.

"You're doing it again." Kyle's voice knocked at the periphery of my thoughts.

When I finally looked at him, he nodded at the empty cups lined up on the counter. I picked up the first one, forcing myself to stop daydreaming.

"C'mon, Jess." Kyle stared at me with those serious eyes of his. Eyes that really should be illegal on a guy you weren't ever going to sleep with. "We both know David was a complete jerk. Besides, you're too good for him, anyway."

Choosing not to answer, I read the scribbled instructions on the side and concentrated on making a soy latte.

As I placed the lid on the cup, I got a whiff of something strong, a smell that wasn't normally in the place. It reminded me of freshly squeezed lemon juice, but not quite. And it was sort of musky, but that wasn't it either.

"I'm just worried about you, that's all," Kyle said.

"I'll be…" I stumbled sideways, grabbing onto the counter. The room steadied beneath my feet.

Kyle squeezed my arm. "Do you need your inhaler? Is it in your locker?"

I shook my head. This wasn't an asthma attack. Of that I was sure. I felt jittery as if I'd been given a shot of caffeine into my veins, but my breathing was clear.

"Jessica?" The voice came at me deep and rich, like a cup of espresso.

I looked up. A strange guy in a trench coat stood beside me. It took me a second to realize he was offering me a bottle of sparkling water. He stared directly into my eyes. The blueness of his was almost translucent, mesmerizing. I looked away first, wishing I hadn't. The water sloshed back and forth in the bottle, but his hands were perfectly still.

I was the one shaking.

"Jessica," he repeated, and the fullness of his voice lifted me out of my confusion. But I couldn't say anything. My words sat stubbornly at the back of my throat.

Customers usually registered into my mind the minute they walked in the door. No matter how busy, a quick glance told me he/she/they, a suit, jogger, mom, retired couple. Not only had this guy appeared out of nowhere, I couldn't put a label on him.

Kyle took the water from the stranger and set it on the counter. "Thank you. But I don't think this is what she needs."

How could Kyle know what I needed? I didn't even know myself.

Trench Coat's piercing gaze sent a rippling effect down my spine. Before I could speak, he turned away.

"You should go sit down," Kyle said. "You don't look right."

I took a deep, clear breath, pressing my palm against my throat. "Where'd he go?" The minute I asked, I saw him in the corner of The Mud Hut, at the table closest to the restrooms.

"And please don't life coach me, Kyle," I said.

His eyebrows dipped downward over his eyes. I had definitely hurt his feelings, which is not what I had meant do to.

But Kyle doesn't give up easily. He's not only my best friend but he's the only one who held me together after David broke off our engagement last year. "Why don't you take a break," he said. "Here comes Nola. She'll cover for you."

"Sure," Nola said, rubbing my back as if I were one of her toddler twins in need of soothing. "You do look sort of pale. Are you feeling weak?"

I shook my head. Quite the contrary. Energy buzzed through my veins. But rather than argue with Nola, whom I adore, I took her advice and sat at a table near the front door, where I had a view of the strange guy.

He clasped his hands, thumbs pressed together and sat completely still. After several minutes, he slowly slipped his arms from his coat.

He wore a short-sleeved shirt, revealing well-muscled arms.

Watching him, I felt a rush of adrenalin, unlike anything I'd ever felt before.

The door opened, and group of yoga women walked in. They swarmed the counter like a bunch of bees instead of forming a line. Kyle and Nola worked in rhythm with each other, taking orders, making the lattes and non-fat cappuccinos.

I thought about going back to my position, but they had it under control. So, inconspicuously I stared at the strange guy. Bubbles of excitement fluttered along my skin every time he glanced in my direction.

He looked about my age, that milestone of thirty reminding me it was time to find my place in life.

His brownish-blond hair waved over his ears and touched the top of his collar. He had a short beard, as if he hadn't shaved in a few days. And there was nothing really wrong with his nose or any other part of his face, when I looked at each feature separately. But there was something not right about the whole picture.

Every few seconds, his hands shimmered. I tried to see if he was holding some kind of light. As far as I could tell, he wasn't. I looked around at the other guests. Everyone else appeared normal.

He kept his back straight, his arms close to his sides, and his head down, staring at his odd-shaped tablet, more oval than square.

His presence moved me into a place I had never been before. I imagined him kissing me, my thoughts circling themselves, like a never-ending roll of film.

This was totally not me thinking. Not the rational me who had sworn off relationships. I couldn't stand it any longer. I got up and walked in his direction, stopping several feet before reaching his table, thinking he would look up. He didn't.

I couldn't talk to him. I literally couldn't move forward. If I went any closer, I was sure my legs would give out. I turned around and headed back to my station.

"That guy is strange," Kyle said. "I don't like the way he's staring at you."

My heart did a little flip.

"I'm going to go talk to him." Kyle squeezed the wet rag in his hand. "See what he's all about." He slapped the rag on the counter and walked toward the break room.

"Ask him how he knew my name?" I said.

Kyle held up the back of his hand at my request.

Seconds later, he emerged in the customer area and marched toward the stranger, my heart beating in time to his footsteps.

Kyle. If you looked his name up on Wikipedia, you'd find the words kind, considerate, intuitive, higher than normal energy aura, dedicated. But there would be this footnote stating, "Not Jessica's type." Which is a good thing, because I love having him as my best friend.

Years ago, after getting partnered in Psych 101, we went on two dates, realized we were better as friends, and here we are. Since David, Kyle's been wanting to try again. I read it in his body language and how he's always trying to please me. But although I never understood the Periodic Table, I know chemistry can't be forced.

While Kyle and Trench Coat talked, I went through

the motions of making a grande frappaccino. Next to the stranger, Kyle appeared awkward and out of place. An utterly unrealistic thought.

But nothing about this morning was normal.

I alternated between looking down, looking up, trying to lip-read. Kyle said "hi" that was easy to figure out and then "Can I get you something?" A bit harder, but discernible.

But when Trench Coat answered, he turned his whole body away from me. Lip-reading became impossible.

I was making my third ice-blended mocha, trying hard not to mess up whipped cream on two, hold it on the third when Kyle finally got back.

"What did you find out?" I set the drinks on the counter and called out, "Susan."

"He's says he's a reporter," Kyle said, relieving Nola at the register. "I think he's full of shit."

"Did you ask him how he knew my name?" I poured soy milk into the next cup before I realized it was supposed to be non-fat.

"I told him you were my girlfriend."

"You what?" My hand jerked, knocking the container of non-fat milk. I caught it before it tipped over.

"Listen, Jess. You said he made you feel uncomfortable. Maybe now he won't come back."

"I said he was strange, that's all. You're strange, too, you know." I glanced down at the sole-less shoes he was always wearing in order to keep microwaves and toasters from going all wonky.

Kyle gave me one of his I can't help it looks, where he turns his lips down and tilts his head like a sad puppy. I know he can't help what he does.

He had explained his condition to me when we first met. Everyone has electrical currents running through their body. His run at a higher-than-normal level. Battery operated watches drain quickly on his wrist. And every year he needs a new cell phone.

And then there is that zing that passes through my body when we touch.

I'm usually sympathetic to his situation. But today, his currents may be high, but my patience was running low.

I placed a top on the non-fat latte and set it on the counter, harder than necessary. A few drops spilled out the opening.

Kyle glanced at me quickly, then turned back to the lady in front of him. "Ma'am, did you say a lemon muffin?"

Hearing papers rustling, I turned in the direction of Trench Coat. He held a thin piece of paper between his fingers. He looked up, and I glanced away quickly.

I concentrated on wiping down my wand. When I could see my face in the shiny silver, I set the towel down and leaned against the counter. My body felt too angular, as if I were made of sharp corners and not smooth skin over curvy hips and thighs.

"You should go home." Nola tapped my arm and gave me a look that said she'd been trying to get my attention.

Part of me wanted to bolt and run straight for next year. Another part of me wanted to stay. That guy did something to me. Something I'd never felt in my entire life. And I craved more of whatever it was.

Shaking off Nola's suggestion, I started on a venti

mocha frappe when the scraping sound tunneled its way toward me. Trench Coat scooted his chair back and stood up.

The cuffs on his button-down shirt were too long. His jeans, which hugged his muscled thighs, seemed old and worn. My mind jumped to the racks at our local thrift shop, a place I knew quite well, given my financial situation.

He curled his fingers into fists. Then stretched them apart, repeating this action several times. After stretching his neck from side to side, he packed up his stuff, put on his long tan coat. A few minutes later, the door opened, and he walked out.

Or had he? The outline of his body hung in the air.

It was faint, but detectable. With my hand out, I rushed toward Trench Coat's image. By the time I reached the door, it faded away. Completely.

"Hey, Jess." Nola nudged my arm. "What are you reaching for?"

I turned around. As I untied my apron, I realized my hands were shaking.

"You looked like you were grabbing something," she said. "You better lay off the caffeine."

"I think I'm going to clock out. Ashley starts soon. You're good, right?"

"Sure. Get some rest," Nola said, rubbing my back.

I hurried into the employee room for my bag. Kyle was waiting for me, with his phone in one hand and his keys dangling in the other. "C'mon. I'm on break. I'll give you a ride home."

That would leave Nola alone, but I wasn't in the mood to argue.

As we crossed the parking lot, I looked around for

the strange guy.

"We sure get all kinds of crazies here," Kyle said, unlocking the passenger side of his truck.

"I thought it was sweet of him to bring me that water." I climbed in and tucked my legs under my butt.

Kyle made an annoying tsking sound.

"Can I ask you something?" I said, while Kyle started the truck. "Was there anything weird to you about how he looked?"

"Besides the way he was gawking at you?"

"No, I mean. He was solid, right?"

"What are you getting at?" Kyle zoomed out of the lot and into the oncoming traffic.

I grabbed onto the handle over the door. "Do you have to drive so fast?"

"No." He grinned at me. "What are you doing later? I'm off at three."

I thought about bringing up how the guy had shimmered, but obviously, Kyle hadn't noticed it, so I let it go.

"How about a movie?" he asked, after he parked the truck.

A movie sounded great. Something that might get me excited about film school again. And I desperately needed inspiration if I was ever going to move on with my life.

The word temporary in my job description had morphed into permanent months ago.

But I couldn't stop thinking about that guy long enough to concentrate on what Kyle was saying, let alone a movie.

"Three-fifteen sound good? I'll pick you up after work."

"Not today," I said.

"Tell me you're working on your screenplay, and I'll let you off easy."

"I wish. I haven't even had one idea since David." I stopped talking, realizing I actually said his name without feeling that avalanche press against my chest.

"You never know what's going to happen next, Jess. Inspiration could be right around the corner, at the movies."

"Nice try, coach…but not today."

"Gotcha." Kyle squeezed my hand, causing that slight electrical zing between us. "Just my animal magnetism," he teased.

I pulled my hand onto my lap.

The only car in our driveway was my transmission-less Honda Civic, which meant my grandparents were running their Tuesday errands.

I was two paychecks away from finally getting it fixed. My grandmother had offered to help, but I've taken too much from them already. And besides, I'd made a promise to myself to become self-sufficient by the age of thirty. It was enough that I lived rent free in the studio apartment attached to the back of their house.

On the pretense that he needed to use the bathroom, Kyle parked his truck and followed me through the front door.

While he went off to the bathroom, I read the note my grandmother had left on the kitchen table. *At the dry cleaners and library. Not going to the market today. Xoxoxox.*

We've been leaving each other notes since forever.

Kyle emerged from the bathroom with a pleading look on his face. "I can't change your mind about later?" he asked, pouring himself a glass of water.
I shook my head. "Not today." I took the glass from his hands, set it on the counter and led him to the front door.

As we were saying goodbye, Kyle's phone beeped.

"It's Heather," he said, reading the text message. Two seconds later, his phone rang. He let it go to voicemail. But it rang again before we said goodbye.

"You better get it," I said.

As I shut the door, I could hear Kyle talking.

"Listen, Heather…"

Heather is Kyle's ex. They broke up over a month ago. But for the past few days she's been calling nonstop. Kyle's been trying to make their break-up a "nice thing" after watching how David had treated me, but let's be honest, how nice can breaking up be? Someone always ends up getting hurt.

Personally, I think they make a great couple, but my opinion isn't worth much.

Just as my grandparents don't care that I think it's time to stop worrying about my financial situation and spend their money on themselves. I've been suggesting home improvements for years, but my grandmother is as stubborn as a coffee stain.

The carpets in their main house resemble something from a horror movie, a drab avocado green. The flowery wallpaper is cracked and peeling. And water drains from the washing machine into the bathtub on the other side of the wall. But Grandma loves this place.

I crossed the kitchen and opened the door to my

studio apartment. After pulling open the curtains, letting the sunlight fall onto my unmade bed, I lit a vanilla candle and flopped down on the comforter with my mail.

There was an invitation to yet another wedding shower. At least I wasn't a bridesmaid. Again. A credit card invitation. Just what I didn't need. A catalog showing overpriced yoga clothes. The last envelope was from my film advisor. The last chance I had to succeed.

I had wanted to make movies as far back as I could remember. Instead of following my dream, for fear of failure, I went to community college and got my AA. It had taken me four years to finish a two-year program. I should have known I was going down the wrong path.

But I was in my early twenties with time on my side. I figured I would waitress and write on the side. And then I met David. If nothing else, he convinced me to apply to film school.

Not yet ready to deal with Mr. Moore, I tossed the letter aside.

Then I did what I always do when I'm bothered by something. I picked up the stack of postcards from my father which I keep on my nightstand next to my journal.

He's been sending them since I was eight, when he started acting in all those corny western movies made over in Europe. Reading his signature, XOXOXO Pa, usually puts me in a good mood. But not today.

I couldn't get my mind off that guy, off how his image stayed in the room after he had already left.

But it was more than that. He had left some sort of footprint on my psyche. The whole time he had been in

The Hut, I had found it hard to concentrate without looking up at him while making the drinks. And his smell, that lemony scent, would hit me every few minutes.

I rose from my bed, tearing open the envelope from Mr. Moore. Just what I figured.

"Dear Jessica,

I have not yet received the topic for your final film. As you know this is a requirement for graduation. Please let me know by the end of the month if you plan on continuing with our program."

I tossed the letter onto my dresser.

After changing out of my work clothes, I went through the main house and left a note for my grandmother. *Going over to Aunt Beth's.*

Walking down the block, I thought of Trench Coat. His eyes, so captivating. He'd looked at me as if he knew things about me. Or maybe, I wanted him to know me. Logically, it made no sense at all. But my heart knew exactly what it wanted.

Chapter Two

A matchmaker must record his findings within three hours of meeting the subject of his mission. Law #7.

Renn paced the sidewalk across the street from The Mud Hut, repeating this most important law from the *Time Traveling Matchmaker's Handbook.*

Alongside his own whisperings, he heard Arlianna's voice. He pictured his mentor's lips enunciating each word as she twirled a long curly strand of hair around her forefinger. He knew it was crucial to follow the laws. He knew he could be terminated. He knew his future could be ruined. He also knew something, something strong prohibited him from sending the data.

For two hours and fifty minutes, he'd been thinking only about Jessica, the subject of his mission. Nothing else had occupied his mind.

"You're meant for this job," Arlianna had said how many times in the past few months? "You're a natural. And Time Traveling Matchmakers Inc. is made better by your talents."

Where were those talents now? He'd even lost his core for a second or two back in the coffee shop. Natural born time travelers were not supposed to lose their balance.

If he didn't get the data recorded in the next ten

minutes, he'll have failed his first solo mission.

He opened his tablet to page one of his log.

From the log of Renn Porter, Apprentice Matchmaker.

Mentor: Arlianna Greenhouse

Mission# 265 – Griffin & Singleton

Mission: Locate & Return (L&R) w/ Jessica Dylan Singleton (JDS)

Dest: The Mud Hut, Northridge, CA 7.24.Present Day.

Avatar of JDS: Hair-Ash Blonde

Eyes- Green

Complex: Creamy

Age: 29.8

Blood Type – B Neg

Apps: Yoga, swimming, snowboarding

Aspir: Current—Film directing

Past-Chef, to be a good wife someday

Edu: HS grad w/ honors

AA- Business

LA Film School—Currently enrolled

FamHist: Mother-deceased

Father – Actor

Lives in apt attached to home of Gma & Gpa

Close with Aunt and Uncle

Pers Type: INTP

Foods: Sushi, Pasta

Highs: Movies

Lows: Insecure

Day One

Arrived at set dest at exactly 7.24

JDS in distress

Stabilized CORE

Assumed coverup with co-worker. CW has int in JDS. Neg on the return.

Various smiles: Flirty, trusting, curious

Overall demeanor: Charming, alluring, underlying sexiness

Observation period: 2hrs 10 min

Departed for home base

Met w/ Arlianna

Followed JDS home.

Followed JDS to Ant & Unc.

Add'l notes:

At times CORE functioned 85% -unnat behavior. Why?

I fear detachment of residue

Had convo w/Arlianna to discuss this sit. She suggests further observ, possible flaws in calculation could be the cause.

Submitted: 4:30 PM

****

Aunt Beth was thirty when that drunk driver crashed into Mom's car. Uncle Joe wasn't Uncle Joe yet. But Mom's death left a big gaping hole in Aunt Beth's heart, and he stepped in to fill the void. All of ours, actually. Not that anyone could ever take the place of a mom, a sister, or a daughter, but Uncle Joe fell into our family so seamlessly, it was like he belonged there.

I know my aunt and uncle wanted kids, but that didn't happen for them. They had plans to travel. That didn't happen, either.

Until now. And my uncle's idea was so out-there-crazy. Crazier than anything he's ever done. And ridiculous if you ask me.

Why Aunt Beth kept saying she needed to stand by

him drove me insane. I was never going to stand by a guy again as long as I lived. I had wasted 755 days with David, pretending to like horror films, car museums, and believing that he really wanted to get married.

Our breakup shattered me into a million pieces. And I was still trying to glue myself back together.

As I walked, I replayed the events of the morning. That faint image of the stranger lingered in my mind. Nola had to be right. Too much caffeine after too little sleep can play havoc on the imagination.

I crossed the light and turned into my aunt's neighborhood.

This is my favorite part of the walk. It's a tree-lined street, about five blocks long. The houses are small, but everyone has a welcoming porch.

Halfway down the street, I felt someone behind me. I turned around expecting to see one of the little kids who are always riding their bikes or jump roping. There was no one there.

But the minute I started walking again a light mist tickled the back of my legs. My heartbeat quickened.

I turned around again. Nothing. Still, my body knew something wasn't right. My legs moved faster.

As I reached my aunt's street, two figures appeared in front of the house at the far end of her block.

Both in trench coats. One was the guy from The Mud Hut. The other figure stood a few inches shorter with a mass of curly hair. My mind conjured up those spies in the movies David always dragged me to.

I stopped mid-step, my heart knocking on my chest, watching as they moved farther away. Watching as their coats glimmered in the afternoon sun. This was not my imagination.

After a few seconds, adrenalin swelled inside me, propelling me forward. "Hey! Stop!"

They kept on walking and turned the corner.

A second or two later I reached the spot where I had last seen them, expecting to still see them farther down the block.

They were gone. In their place hung a wispy cloud, similar to that image I had seen earlier at work. There had been two people walking, of that I was certain, yet I only saw one outline. That of the guy.

I moved toward the shape, hovering about two feet above the sidewalk. As I stepped into it, the sky felt as if it lay on my shoulders, heavy and ominous.

I hunched forward, breathing quickly through my mouth.

Seconds later, the pressure disappeared along with the image. I looked at my hands and arms and down at the sidewalk. I stomped my foot. The ground was solid. Concrete.

I walked up the block checking every porch, although I knew I wasn't going to find them.

I turned around, moving slowly at first, and then my muscles kicked into action. I ran at full speed to my aunt's house. All the while, feeling, knowing, someone watched me.

Aunt Beth opened the door as I ran up the driveway. Most of her thick, brown hair was held back off her face by a turquoise clip I had given her for her birthday last year.

"What's wrong?" she asked, blowing on a stray hair. "Is it Grandpa?"

I shook my head.

"Grandma?" Her voice rose into the air.

"They're good." I wheezed as I caught my breath, bending over with my hands on my thighs.

My aunt placed her hand on my shoulder. "You look scared to death."

I grabbed her arm and followed her into the house.

As always, her kitchen felt like my second home, actually my third. Even though it's been a long time, I still have a few memories of the house where I lived with my parents. Or maybe it was the cucumber scented candle on her windowsill, a smell that always evoked my mother's touch.

A bouquet of half-opened daffodils sat on the counter, next to an open bottle of red wine.

The small TV in the corner was on without the sound. The news lady was talking very seriously about something that was happening in another country. Behind her there was a map of Europe.

I was glad the sound was off. Not that I don't care about the world. But at the moment, I just cared more about mine. It loomed in front of me like one gigantic landscape of confusion.

Aunt Beth poured herself a glass of wine, and then held up the bottle offering me a glass.

I shook my head. The last thing I needed now was to alter an already shaky reality.

After taking a sip, Aunt Beth picked up my hand, squeezing my fingers as she studied my face.

I chewed on the inside of my cheek, almost wishing this was another David sighting episode. At least that was founded in reality. What I had just witnessed could have been a scene from one of Uncle Joe's sci fi movies.

"Jessie, tell me what's wrong."

Images raced across my mind, erasing her words.

"Jessie. Earth to Jessie." Aunt Beth snapped her fingers in front of my face.

Her voice pulled me back to the kitchen. "I'm losing it," I whispered.

"What happened?"

Looking in my aunt's eyes, I felt just as I had all those years ago after my Mom died—helpless and scared. I wanted so badly for her to believe what I was going to tell her.

Aunt Beth picked up her glass and carried it to the kitchen table. Before saying anything else, I sat down like I've been doing all my life.

And like she's been doing forever, Aunt Beth sat down beside me, placing her elbows on the table, resting her head in her hands.

"I'm seeing things," I said. Aunt Beth's face remained expressionless. "Like the shapes of people after they're not there anymore."

"Can you be a little more specific? What do mean by shapes?"

There was no judgment in her voice. There never is.

By the time I finished telling Aunt Beth about Trench Coat, her face had tightened into her worried look, and she reached for my hand.

"Do you think it's from something I ate?" I asked her. "Or from too much coffee?" I bit the inside of my cheek. "Why do you think this is happening?"

"Stop that." She pulled her hand out of mine and tapped my cheek. "Let me ask you one question, and don't get mad. You haven't done any drugs, have you?"

"No, of course not. How could you even think

that?" I tried to keep the anger out of my voice, but it crept in like a draft of wind seeping under a doorway. I immediately felt sorry for my harsh words.

"No worries," I went on. "I'd probably think the same thing if someone told me what I just told you."

"Well, then, I think you're just tired."

"He knew my name, Aunt Beth."

"He probably heard someone calling you," she said.

"Okay, then, explain why he was here, on your block?"

"But you didn't see his face. Maybe it wasn't him."

"No, but I saw that same after image thing. And how many people wear a trench coat in Southern California?"

"Hmmm…" Taking a sip of her wine, Aunt Beth blinked a few times, the way she does when she doesn't really know what to say. But then her eyes were sort of red, so maybe her contacts were bothering her. "You sure you don't want some?" She raised her glass in the air.

"Positive."

"It could have been an illusion," she went on. "The way the sun hit their jackets. Reflection off the trees or something. When we're upset, our minds do funny things."

I wanted to believe her explanations, but what I had seen had been too real. "I guess it's possible," I said, knowing that was what she wanted to hear.

"And you have been upset, honey. I assume you haven't gotten your car fixed yet?"

"No. Pretty soon."

"Well, between that problem and David, plus

helping Grandma… Speaking of pressure, did you write your advisor yet?" She refilled her wine glass.

"No." I let out a breath of air.

"It'll come to you. And you know what? One day you're going to wake up, and David won't even be on your mind." Her eyes showed the beginning of a smile.

Which made me start to smile, too. Aunt Beth had an infectious way about her. She's always been able to make me feel better. I guess that's because she's the one who spent the most time with me after Mom's accident.

I've tried to always be there for her, too, but most of the time I fall short, letting my own problems take over. Like now.

"So, what's going on with you and Uncle Joe?" I asked, making a conscious effort to not think about my life.

"I guess I'm going with him."

"Do you really want to?" I asked.

"No. But he's my husband. For better or worse, right?"

"Maybe I should go, too." I bit on the inside of my cheek. "Africa doesn't sound like much fun, but I'll be away from here."

"Here isn't so bad. And whatever happened today at work probably won't happen again."

"Here's the thing, Aunt Beth. As much as it freaked me out, I want to see him again. I was totally shocked to see him on your street. But excited at the same time."

"Maybe you will," she said. "It's possible he lives around here."

"Why didn't he stop when I called?"

"He might not have heard you."

"You have an answer for everything, don't you?" I smiled. This was so like my aunt.

"Not everything. Tell me about him. What does he look like?"

"He's sexy in a gritty sort of way, with a stubbly beard and longish hair." I ran my hand over my chin. "He was like…I can't explain." And I really couldn't. It was a feeling I couldn't catch. But I could feel it in my mind, like waking up in the middle of a dream and trying to remember all the details. "I was drawn to him. Like nothing I've ever felt before."

"See, you're already getting over David. You want dinner?"

She walked to the fridge, opening and closing the door a few times. "How about if we go to the deli. Do you need to get home?"

I was in a hurry to become self-sufficient. To become whatever I was supposed to be in life. But I was never in a hurry to leave my aunt.

Chapter Three

By the time Aunt Beth dropped me at home, the lights were out in the main house. Instead of getting to my apartment through my grandparents' kitchen, I went through the backyard to my private door. The branches on our Chinese Elm hung low, brushing against my cheek as I passed under her massive girth.

"It's been a crazy day," I said to the tree. Of course, I knew she couldn't answer. But I like to think she does hear me. I talk to her all the time and have ever since Mom died.

In those early days, I truly believed she did talk to me. When it was windy, she spoke to me in melodies. In the heat, her words were crisp and short.

I spent hours sitting with my back against her trunk, watering her with my tears.

"I met this guy. He's weirdly wonderful if that makes sense."

Her branched dipped lower as if she understood. I rubbed one of her leaves, and then entered my tiny studio.

The first thing I always see when I step through the door are the two framed photos sitting on my dresser. One is of my mom and dad sitting on a picnic bench. My dad is holding a beer, and my mom is touching the pearl necklace my dad had given her for her birthday. I ran my finger along my neckbone, wishing I hadn't lost the pearl that day at the beach. If not for David I might have found it. But he'd been so annoyed, dragging me away from the sand after I'd been searching for a half hour. I should have left him right then.

The other is the three of us, taken when I was six, about two weeks before Mom died. My parents are each kissing one of my cheeks, but their eyes are on each other.

I picked up both the photos and pressed them to my chest as I lay down on top of the covers.

The dusty blades on the ceiling fan cut through the air. Not for the first time, I thought how my life had been divided into sections.

Act one ~*~ Living with Mom and Dad until…fade out… I squeezed my eyes tight until the monstrous hurt in my chest subsided. Act two ~*~ Growing up, becoming who I am, planning and watching my future fall apart. Act three ~*~ Picking up the pieces. Aren't there only supposed to be three acts to a good screenplay?

Was this how it was going to be from now on?

Sometime around two in the morning, I finally fell asleep and woke up seven hours later under the covers to the sound of the wake-up chimes on my phone. I pulled it from the charger and saw a text message from Kyle asking if I needed a ride to work.

No, I typed.

Accepting a ride would give me more time to get ready, but I felt like walking. I flung my feet to the ground and walked into my mini kitchen, which had a microwave and a coffee maker on the counter, a three-foot refrigerator, and a sink. I popped in a K-cup, pushed start, and headed for the bathroom. Two quick raps followed by a third stopped me—my grandmother's signature knock.

"Come in," I called.

She carried her favorite mug with the word LOVE emblazoned on the side and sat down at the table across from my bed.

"Good morning, sweetie," Grandma said, taking a sip of her coffee. "Would it be too much bother for you to drop off my prescription on your way to work?" She pulled a slip of paper from her bathrobe pocket and set it on my dresser.

"No, of course not," I said, taking my cup from the maker and adding a splash of cream. On the way to the table, I picked up the photos that had fallen to the floor and set them back on the dresser. "I wish Dad would meet someone else. Has he even been on a date?"

"They were soulmates," Grandma said, walking over to the photos. She picked up the one of my parents on the park bench and traced Mom's hairline with her finger. It took a few minutes before she said anything. "There was something special about them."

My inner six-year-old fixated on the memory of that day. As we walked, hand in hand, I imagined the three of us held together by puppet strings. I thought my parents were perfect and perfect for each other. As long as it was the three of us, the world was a safe, happy place.

"I remember the way they used to laugh," I said.

"Your father brought out the best in your mom." Grandma set the photo on the dresser and sat down across from me. "After he showed up, crazy as it was saying he didn't remember anything about his life or even his name, your mom changed. Little stuff didn't bother her anymore. She started reading about ESP and all that paranormal stuff."

"How come they didn't want to know what was wrong with him?"

"It stopped mattering. They were quite a couple. Your mom and dad."

"I think about her every day," I said.

"I do, too." Grandma gave me that knowing smile, the one I love more than anything in the world. "I better go check on your grandfather."

As she leaned over and kissed me on the forehead, her lavender scent washed over me like a warm blanket. "We're going to our discussion group. And then Grandpa has a doctor appointment," she said. "It'll be a long day for him."

"I'll cook tonight, then, okay? I'll make Grandpa's favorite pasta."

She smiled at me and nodded her head the tiniest little bit.

My grandmother was sixty when that drunk driver crashed into Mom's car. I know it tore her apart, but she had to keep it all together and become the mom of a little girl all over again. Lots of people actually thought she was my mom because she looked so young. And because we look so much alike, with our wavy hair, green eyes, and small bones.

But now, watching her leave with my dirty T-shirts, I could see that my grandmother wasn't so young anymore.

"Grandma," I called out. "I love you."

"Well, I love you, too."

After she left, I looked through my closet for something to wear. That awful Mud Hut apron hides everything, so I usually don't care. But knowing, hoping, Renn would show up, I wanted to wear something flattering.

****

There was no one at the pharmacy counter, not even the pharmacist. I tapped my fingers on the Chapstick display, leaning forward to see if anyone was in between all the rows of prescriptions waiting to be picked up. We would never leave the counter unattended at work. Especially not with our tip jar there for everyone to see.

That same misty feeling as yesterday creeped over me, tickling the back of my legs. A strip of darkness flashed in my peripheral vision. Turning around quickly, I saw a lady in a trench coat identical to the one Renn had been wearing. She held a bottle of pills, turning it slowly from side to side.

I knew immediately that it wasn't the same woman I had seen yesterday. But the churning in my gut told me they were related.

This lady had dark hair pulled back in a ponytail, making her appear austere and hard. Whereas the woman from yesterday had moved fluidly down the street, this woman appeared stiff, mannequin-like, as she lifted her head in my direction.

Something moved near the side of her face. No, it was on her face. It looked like a tattoo. I squinted, trying to get a better look. The design changed from a heart to a silhouette of two heads.

I must have made some kind of sound because the old man behind me in line asked if I was okay.

I put my hand over my mouth, as if that would stop my heart from beating so fast. Was she going to shimmer?

Her crimson lips were ruler straight. Her eyes remained dark and unmoving.

"Can I help you?" The voice came from my left.

I turned to face the white-haired man I had forgotten was there.

"What?"

"I didn't say anything," he answered.

"Did you want to leave that?" Now the voice came from in front of me.

"What?"

"Are you leaving a prescription?" The pharmacist motioned toward the paper in my hand.

"Uh…yeah," I said, thrusting it at him.

When I turned to check on the woman, she was gone.

I hurried from the pharmacy counter and through the store. She was nowhere in sight.

"Hey, watch it," a mother pushing a stroller said as I bumped into her.

"Sorry," I mumbled.

But then I had to catch myself before knocking into an old woman.

"Are you all right, young lady?" The woman asked, with the same concern that my grandmother had in her voice this morning.

"Fine, fine," I said.

"Maybe you should just sit here a minute and rest," the lady suggested.

"No, no, I'm fine. Honest."

When I left the drugstore, I started toward home. I made it halfway down the block before I realized I was supposed to be going to work.

For a split second I thought of crawling back in bed. But what good would that do?

****

"Get a grip," I said as I shoved my purse in my preschool sized cubbyhole. "If he shows up, which I hope he does, I'm just going to ask him about yesterday."

"Who are you talking to?" Nola asked, startling me.

"Myself."

"You better tell yourself to hurry. Some kind of tourist bus with a bunch of old people just pulled up outside." Nola slung her bag under a bench, smiled at herself in the mirror hanging on the back of the door, and rushed off.

I tied my apron around my waist, pulled my hair back in a ponytail, and followed her to our work stations.

I groaned at the sight of the crowd, hoping no one wanted anything more than a plain drip coffee. And that they made their choices quickly.

The first man in line held up an old digital camera and asked me to smile. The badge on his shirt read "Dan M. Santa Barbara Coastline Senior Center."

Who would have thought The Mud Hut would be a tourist attraction?

I was in the middle of squirting whipped cream into a cup of black coffee for one of my regulars, who managed to make his way to the front of the line, when the lemony scent drifted toward me. I gripped the can harder to stop my hand from shaking.

"Hey, that's enough, Jessie." *Black with Whip* held out his hand.

As I put on the lid, foam spilled over the top and onto the counter.

"Sorry." I handed him his drink, trying to keep it together. Trying not to let my hands shake. At least, my breathing was okay. For now.

Trench Coat sat down at the same table as yesterday. He pulled out that same oblong tablet and started typing.

My heart beat to the rhythm of his fingers.

"Cover for me, will you?" I asked Nola.

I walked off without waiting for her answer.

If he knew I stood beside his table, he didn't acknowledge my presence. Not at first.

My full name—Jessica Dylan Singleton—was displayed in bold letters at the top of his tablet screen. Directly beneath my name the word *Flaws* flashed on and off.

Without saying anything he quickly pressed a button making his screen go dark.

There was absolutely no way he heard anyone at The Hut call me by first and last name, let alone know my middle name. And the way he hid what he was typing reminded me of how David would react when I walked in on him texting his co-worker/secret lover.

I steadied myself ready to confront him. The instant he looked up, I forgot everything I was going to say. It didn't seem to matter anymore.

I couldn't stop staring at his eyes. I'd never seen any that blue, trimmed with light mocha.

But it was more than just their color. It was the way he looked at me, as if, well, I know it sounds crazy, but as if he had been expecting me for a long time.

He drank in every bit of my face. My cheeks grew

hot. I clasped my hands together and pressed them to my chest.

"Hello." All the chatter and noise in the room parted as his one single word, deep and rich, made its way toward me.

"Hi." My voice came out unrecognizable to myself.

"Hello," he said again, crossing his arms and leaning back in the chair.

"Hi," I repeated. The words that usually poured out of me fell to the cutting room floor.

When he smiled, a small dimple formed in his cheek. "I'm assuming you didn't come to take my order."

I shook my head, mesmerized by his eyes.

"I, um…I…was wondering, do you live near here?" Oh God, I might as well have been asking about his sun sign.

"Why do you ask?"

"Um, just curious. I thought I saw you walking yesterday and…"

"It wasn't me," he said, looking down.

"I didn't even tell you where I was."

He started blinking, a sure sign of lying according to my aunt.

I pulled out a chair from the empty table next to his, and as I sat down brushed my hand against his coat draped over the back of his seat.

It had a watery feel to it. A dampness covered my fingers.

"I saw someone walking in this coat and…" As I reached to touch it again, a faint blue mist rose into the air. He pulled it onto his lap, moving it out of my reach.

"And?" He settled his hand next to mine on the

table. The space between our fingers charged with electricity. I had to concentrate on not reaching out and taking his hand.

"It's just odd, that's all. It's pretty warm for a coat this heavy, don't you think?"

"To each his own, Jessica." He carried out the S sound, letting the last half of my name rest on his tongue.

"How do you know my name?"

"I heard that guy, your friend, use it."

"No, you didn't," I said. "He never calls me Jessica."

"He should. I like it better. I'm Renn." He held out his hand. "Renn Porter."

I grasped his hand firmly and let go quickly, afraid if I didn't, I might hold on forever.

As our fingers separated, I heard Nola calling me.

"See." I nodded toward the register. "Everyone calls me Jessie."

"You better get back to work," he said.

My body tingled all over, more intense than it had yesterday.

He put on his coat and pressed his hands against the table, pushing back his chair. That's when I saw it. Again. The shimmering. And his hands sort of sliding through the table.

"Are you working tomorrow?" he asked, as if nothing unusual was going on. Or maybe it wasn't. Maybe I was just seeing things again.

I barely nodded.

"Cool. See ya then." That outdated slang expression sounded even odder coming from him.

I stared at his back as he walked out the door,

33

waiting for the after-image I had seen yesterday. But it didn't appear.

And I know it sounds weird, but my heart did that shifting thing again, and it felt like part of my soul walked out the door with him.

A few minutes after he left, as I moved slowly toward my station at the bar, Kyle burst into The Mud Hut like an avalanche.

"What's wrong?" I asked, suspecting something must have happened with Heather.

"Nola texted he was here again."

"It's all good," I said.

I glanced over at Nola, busy ringing up a sale. Getting angry at her wouldn't change anything. I let it go and started cleaning the wands and counter.

A flurry of tan rushed by the window. Renn paced back and forth.

"Why is he out there?" Kyle asked.

I slapped my rag on the countertop. "Be right back."

Before Kyle could stop me, I lifted the counter up and walked into the customer area.

A group of women in workout clothes streamed through the door. The kind who spend more time on how they look than how they exercise.

While they started rattling off double mochas, non-fat lattes, caps no foam, I made my way to the exit.

He was gone.

****

A TTMM must have open communication with his mentor during the first twenty-hours of his mission. Law #6.

Renn opened the Memo icon on his tablet and

tapped Arlianna's face. The screen blinked, ready for his data.

He couldn't get his fingers moving past the date. He couldn't tell his private thoughts to Central Match. Yet he couldn't lie.

Something was off in the calculations. He felt it with every fiber of his being.

God, Jessica was gorgeous. And those eyes. They filled him with a desire he'd never known before. It had taken all his willpower to keep silent. He had wanted to tell her he'd been in her neighborhood. But admitting the truth would have led to further questions, ones he couldn't answer. Not yet.

Arlianna had engraved that law into his mind until it attached itself to every thought. **Never tell the reason for your mission. Law #22**

That was all he wanted to do. Break that damn law and tell her everything. But he couldn't, and he wouldn't until he was certain.

If only Arlianna hadn't appeared while he had been walking. And then forcing him to disappear like that. No wonder Jessica was a mess.

He knew mentors were supposed to make pop arrivals, but she could have waited until now. Until he was sitting on this hard bench, with his stomach agitating as if it were an old-fashioned butter-making churn.

He shut the screen and opened the private one linking him to his mentor. Arlianna was smart. She'd see that Central Match was not included, read quickly, and hit delete.

Mission #265
Confidential Memo

To: Arlianna Greenhouse
From: Renn Porter
Had convo with subject. Unnerving. Confirm on what we spoke of last night. Something wrong with match. Will keep watch. Follow and report back shortly.
Going walking to clear head.
~*~
To: Renn Porter
From: Arlianna Greenhouse
EAT

Renn read her message, hit delete, and shook his head. He did need to eat. He'd read enough case studies about Travelers who ended up in psych wards from lack of nutrients. His research had informed of the unsavory attitudes toward patients in those institutions.

But what to eat?

Sushi was said to be extremely fresh in this time, unlike where he lived. And Arlianna had confirmed that truth during one of their briefings. Sushi it was.

He dug his hand into the pockets of his coat and headed toward the center of the town.

Chapter Four

It was after eleven in London, but I knew Lilly, my best friend since fourth grade, would be working in her darkroom.

I turned the corner and headed toward Mushi Sushi with plans to call Lilly while eating. Halfway toward the restaurant, a whiff of Renn's lemony scent swirled around me.

He stood across the street in front of Maxie's Travel Agency. I stared at the back of his trench coat, pulling my phone from my bag.

With every nerve in my body at attention I punched in speed dial #1, Lilly's number.

She didn't answer. I left a message for her to call me when she got this message. Whatever time.

I tucked my purse closer to my shoulder and headed toward the corner across from the travel agency.

It seemed like forever before the light turned green. I crossed quickly, nodding at Mike, the owner of the newsstand. Music blasted from his old-fashioned boom box. If I ever filmed the documentary I envisioned about low tech guys surviving in a high-tech world. Mike would definitely be featured.

When I was only a few feet from the agency, a little girl and her mom came toward me. The little girl stopped to tie her shoe. She struggled with the bright pink laces, and her mom bent down to help her.

The little girl's giggles were so light and airy, they made me smile. "Thanks, Mommy," she said. "Tomorrow I can do it myself."

Seeing little girls with their moms doesn't make me sad because I had my mom when I was little. It's young women and their moms that I try not to look at.

I often wonder what our relationship would have been like. If she were here now, I'd like to think she would reassure me of my sanity and give a rational explanation to my feelings toward this unusual man.

Renn was walking toward me at a fast pace. Our eyes met. And then from out of nowhere a guy on a bicycle came speeding down the sidewalk.

He clipped Renn's shoulder, pushing him up against me. Renn's coat caught on the buckle of my purse. I heard a rip. More than that—I felt a rip down the center of my body, jagged like a piece of broken glass. Beneath my feet, the sidewalk tilted.

I lost my balance, tripping over my feet. Somehow, I managed not to fall. Once again steady, I turned to find Renn.

This all happened in a less than a second. But in that second Renn was gone. Vanished. Just like that. All that lingered was his lemony scent. And the memory of his hand on my arm.

I didn't see him in either direction. My head throbbed as if something heavy kept knocking into it.

A minute later that same mother and little girl walked past me. I knew before she stopped that the little girl would bend down to tie her shoe.

She giggled, just like before. "Thanks, Mommy," she said. "Tomorrow I can do it myself."

****

Renn knew the minute he spotted Jessica coming toward him, he needed to turn around.

Law #8 All contact with subject must take place in designated area within first week of arrival.

That area was The Mud Hut. He dug his hands into his pockets, prepared to head in the opposite direction when the cyclist knocked into him.

He fell sideways, knowing immediately something was wrong. He kept falling and tumbling. And then floating softly onto sand. Ocean waves crashed in the distance, mingled with laughter and music.

On unsteady legs, he walked toward the sound. Inside a large, white tent, he saw long tables covered with blue tablecloths. Several dozen people milled around, carrying drinks and plates of food. In a far corner, beneath a halo of light, stood a bride and groom.

Renn centered his core, concentrating on the details of the party in order to figure out where he was.

His watch glowed with an incoming message.

Mission #265
Instant Communication
Arlianna: Where the H R U?

He spoke his answer softly. *Not sure. On a beach. Near a wedding.*

Arlianna: When? Type. Don't talk.

Renn: Late 80's. I think. Shoulder pads. Madonna music

Arlianna: Why?

Renn: Not my fault. A strange force booted me away.

Arlianna: Can U get back?

Renn: Not sure

Arlianna: I'll help.

****

I slumped onto the sidewalk, pressing one hand against the back of my neck, trying to stop the pain.

Had I really seen that mom and little girl walk by again? Or had I imagined the entire scene?

Where had Renn gone? It was as if the earth had opened up and swallowed him. Literally. Right before my eyes, he had disappeared, as impossible as it seemed. He was here one minute, gone the next.

Obviously, he hadn't fallen into the sidewalk. But I didn't know what else to do but run my hands up and down the concrete, just in case. I was thinking how crazy I must have looked, when my hand touched a piece of fabric. It was no bigger than a few inches, but I recognized the slippery texture immediately. It was the corner of his coat that had caught on my purse. I tightened my fist around it.

While moving slowly to a standing position, I shoved it into my pocket.

"Hey, Mike." I walked toward the magazine stand. "Did a guy in a trench coat come by here?"

"Not that I know. You okay?"

I nodded that I was, but of course I remained quite the opposite.

Mike wore a tie-dyed T-shirt and jeans, just like always. His long, gray hair was pulled back into a ponytail, just like always.

The peace symbol tattoo on his upper arm made me think of the strange lady from the pharmacy. Her tattoo had been like a hologram on the side of her face. I wondered who did work like that.

I waved goodbye to Mike and continued walking.

The light at the corner turned from red to green. A car honked. The usual city sounds.

The outside world moved forward as if nothing extraordinary had happened.

Perhaps I had lost consciousness for a minute. Maybe there was something in the water at work. How crazy was I to think that? I was hungry, but I've never fainted before from lack of food. Had I taken one of my grandfather's Alzheimer pills this morning instead of my birth control pill? Okay, now I was thinking crazy. We don't even share a bathroom.

Images of Renn rolled through my brain, chasing themselves for some sort of explanation as I hurried down the block to The Mud Hut.

I stood outside the coffee house watching Kyle arrange the condiment counter. His lips pressed in a straight line as if aligning the various containers was the most important thing in the world. He was obviously applying his life-coaching skills to the task.

I pounded on the glass. Kyle looked up and nodded for me to come in. I motioned for him to come outside. I pressed my finger against my cheek and chewed on the already raw skin inside my mouth. He gave me a one-minute sign.

Two of our regulars, *soy lattes,* who worked at the bank across the street, sat at one of the tables. I knew if I made eye contact, they'd start talking to me. So I kept my head down while waiting.

"What's up?" Kyle asked, startling me from behind.

I grabbed his arm, unable to speak.

"What's wrong?"

"The weirdest things just happened." I swallowed.

I took Kyle's hand, ignoring that familiar zing, and pulled him to an empty table at the far end of the patio. "I was by Maxie's, and I saw Renn, and then this guy on a bike pushed him into me. I lost my balance and then he…" I grabbed onto Kyle's arm. "He disappeared. Just like that. He was gone."

"So, he ran off. He's a weird guy."

"He didn't run anywhere. I told you, he disappeared. And this little girl and her mom walked past me, but they had already done that right before the bike guy came by."

Kyle looked at me as if I were crazy. I sounded crazy. What did I expect?

"And look." I pulled the material from my pocket. "This is from his coat."

Kyle lifted the cloth from the palm of my hand. Tiny sparks flew into the air.

"Wow," he said. "Did you see that?"

I not only saw it, energy surged through my body. My pulse quickened. My leg bounced up and down.

"It is sort of weird." He ran his thumb over the material. "Like silk, but not. I'm no fashion expert, but I've never seen material like this before."

The longer he held the fabric, the jitterier I became. "Can I have it, please?" I held out my hand.

With the fabric back in my possession, a calmness settled on my shoulders.

"This proves that he was there," I said, clutching the material.

"If that's really from his coat, but how do you…"

"It is, Kyle. I know. There's some kind of cult thing going on." I bent my head and pressed my hand to my forehead. "In just twenty-four hours, I've seen three people in the same kind of coat."

"I don't know about a cult, Jess. But look at my hand." A tiny blister formed at the base of his ring finger.

"My hands are okay," I said. "It must have something to do with your condition."

"Possibly." He tried to put his arms around me, but I pushed him away.

"If I don't show up for work tomorrow, check the mental institutions, okay? I'm going home."

"I'll drive you," Kyle offered.

Before I could accept, Nola poked her head out the door calling him back to work.

"I'll walk. I don't want you to get fired."

"Yeah, since it's paradise working here." Kyle motioned that he'd be right in. "I'll call you later."

I blew him an air kiss and headed home. I walked quickly, face forward, listening for sounds, my hand clutched around the strange piece of fabric.

Through the living room window, I saw my grandmother in her chair reading a book. She glanced up as I approached.

My grandfather was asleep in his recliner. Frank Sinatra crooned loudly into the air. His low notes vibrated along my skin.

"Hi, sweetheart." My grandmother's smile immediately morphed into a concerned look. "What's wrong?"

"Nothing." I sat down on the ottoman in front of her.

"Did you pick up my pills?"

"Oh, my God, I forgot," I said, pressing my palm to my forehead. It was the first time I've ever forgotten something this important.

"Don't worry." She patted my hand. "I don't need them until tomorrow."

"But I feel horrible. I'll go get them now." But I didn't get up.

"You'll do no such thing. I'll get them tomorrow. Now tell me, what's bothering you?"

I picked at a hole in the stool, avoiding my grandmother's eyes.

Grandma set her book down. "Jessie, what's going on with you?"

I contemplated spilling it all out to her. But it was too crazy a story. Like Kyle said, people don't just vanish. Events don't repeat. People don't shimmer.

"It's nothing, Grandma, really."

"Since when have you kept secrets from me?"

Never.

I bit down on the inside of my cheek, trying to hold back my tears. "Does mental illness run in our family?" My lips wouldn't stop trembling, and the tears just gushed out like a broken fire hydrant.

"Come here." She reached for my hands. Hers was soft and wrinkled. A hand that held mine tightly on the day of my mother's funeral and hasn't let go since. "Tell me, what's the matter?"

"Just horrible customers, that's all."

Grandma knew I was hiding something. "You can tell me all about it when you're ready. I'm not going anywhere."

The words were about to jump out of my mouth when my cell rang. "It's Lilly," I said reading the number.

"Tell her I said hi." Grandma ran a hand through

her short, white hair and then picked up her book.

The minute I heard Lilly's voice, I started rambling about Renn. I almost didn't hear her say that she'd decided to come to her cousin's wedding and would arrive tomorrow.

After hanging up, she sent me a text. —*See you on the porch.*— My spirits lifted reading those words.

****

Holy crap. Renn hadn't even finished reading Arlianna's message when he felt a yanking on his coat. And before he could swallow his fear, he was falling again. He landed in Jessica's neighborhood on that same hard bench where he'd been sitting earlier.

His heart raced as he stabilized his core. He had no freaking idea why this had happened again. He was orbiting out of control. If Central Match found out, he'd be fired.

His locator lit up.

Arlianna's voice sounded as thin as a wisp of her hair. *Send a report. They are waiting.*

He began typing, hiding all emotion from his report. Just the facts, ma'am. He'd heard that saying on an old TV show. Just the facts.

From the log of Renn Porter, Apprentice Matchmaker

Mentor: Arlianna Greenhouse
Mission# 265 – Griffin & Singleton
Day 2 1:19 PM
Spent time with subject. Exch dialogue
Demeanor: Super sensitive, inquisitive, smart
Pln to return in PM for further observ
Diff than expected. Can't explain yet.
Submitted 5:30 PM

Chapter Five

I had a ton of things to accomplish. Not the least being the letter to my advisor. But I couldn't concentrate.

I toyed with the strange fabric, rubbing my thumb over its watery surface. My skin grew cold. Lilly had suggested I practice yoga to relax my mind. I got as far as taking the mat from the closet.

Nothing seemed to clear Renn from my thoughts.

With the strange piece of fabric tucked safely in the side pocket of my purse, I asked my grandmother if I could borrow her car. After she agreed, I headed for The Mud Hut.

Nola's Prius was parked in the employee section of the lot. The only other car was a red Mazda. Tuesday nights were notoriously slow.

I pushed open the door to The Hut, my intention being on getting a latte and talking to Nola. But the second I walked in my plans changed.

Before I even saw him, his lemony scent engulfed me. My nerves jittered as our eyes connected. He looked down quickly. I kept staring.

He sat in the same spot where he had been earlier with his coat draped over the seat next to him.

Nothing shimmered. He was a solid person from head to foot.

On jellyfish legs I walked to his table.

"Hey." I could practically feel my heart opening and closing. Pumping so loud, I was sure Renn could hear its beat.

"Hello," Renn said. He might have been trying to keep his voice steady, but his eyes gave him away. It was just like the first time, as if he'd been waiting for me for forever.

"Can I?" I gestured toward the empty chair.

"Sure." His smile was like the happy ending to a sit-on-the-edge-of-your-seat movie. "I was hoping you'd show up."

"Really?" I stared at his perfectly shaped lips. At his compelling eyes. At his slight beard. I was never one for facial hair, but it looked so damn sexy on him. I wanted to climb onto his lap and press myself against his body. "Well, here I am."

He set his tablet on the table. I tucked my hands under my thighs.

He shifted in his seat, then leaned back with his arms behind his head. I shifted in my seat. The air hung between us, full of pauses and unspoken words.

"Hey, Jess, want a latte?" Nola called out.

"Sure," I said, happy for the distraction. "You want anything?"

"No, thank you."

"Be right back."

I walked over to the counter, feeling Renn's eyes on my butt, thankful I hadn't worn my old, baggy sweatpants.

"How long has he been here?" I whispered to Nola.

"For hours," she said. "He's so strange. I'm glad you showed up. He gives me the creeps, just sitting there. Why are you here, anyway?"

I stole a quick glance at Renn. Because I was drawn here by some magnetic force. And if I don't get to feel his skin against mine, I'm sure to go insane. And because I have to know how he disappears.

"I was bored." I turned my real answer into something Nola wouldn't turn into a tabloid story.

I felt him watching me as I waited for my latte. The few times I turned around, he quickly looked away.

Two regulars came in. *The Green Tea with Sweetener* and her friend, *the Double Pump, Hold the Whip Venti Frap.* They always complain about their drinks, and neither of them ever leaves a tip.

"Not them." Nola twisted her face into a grimace.

"Have fun." I took my latte from Nola and walked back toward Renn.

He had his hands clasped in his lap, twirling his thumbs. I sat down and placed my drink on the table.

"Hello," he said. "Again."

"Hi." I cupped my hand around the warm latte. "Again."

We stared at each other, our faces moving a little closer as the seconds ticked by. A current of energy pulsed between us. I had this unreasonable urge to kiss him. Even though I was scared of who he was or wasn't.

A conversation behind me, something about carbs and tennis shoes, broke whatever thread held us together.

I leaned back in my chair and took a sip of my latte. He was still staring at me when I set it back down, making me feel uncomfortable and yet happy at the same time.

"Listen, Renn," I managed to say. "About earlier."

"I should have just told you." He moved his hands from his lap to the table and started twirling his fingers again. "I'm doing a report on coffeehouses."

"I mean about what happened with the bicycle."

His body stiffened slightly. He avoided my eyes as he reached for his coat. The material made a soft crinkly sound.

"Where did you go?" I asked.

"I had business to take care."

"I mean, you disappeared. You didn't just go around the corner. You...you vanished."

Renn rubbed the back of his neck, avoiding my eyes and my accusation. He didn't seem sure of himself. One thing I did know, he knew exactly what I was talking about.

"Tell me how?"

"Sometimes things happen that we can't explain." He placed his hand next to mine on the table, moving it so that our pinkies touched. Oh, God. Tingles ripped through me. I looked at his long, smooth fingers.

With the other hand he tapped an icon on his tablet, the muscles in his face tightening.

"Is everything okay?" I asked.

He didn't answer.

"Do you need more information for your article?"

He scrunched his eyes. A confused look passed across his face.

"For your coffeehouse piece?"

"Ah." He shook his head. "I'm good."

"Hey, guys." Nola walked past with the condiments. "I'm closing up."

"But it's only 8:30." And I need more time with Renn.

"Tessa called and told me to close."

There was no arguing with our boss and besides, why would Nola want to stay open another hour so I could sit and talk to Renn?

"It's been a pleasure," Renn said. After glancing at his tablet again, he got up and put on his coat. The glow from the overhead light bounced off his shoulders. He reached for my hand and started to say something but then changed his mind. Feeling uneasy, I crossed my arms in front of my chest.

"You're not going to tell me what's really going on, are you? Should we go somewhere private?"

His eyes looked into mine—his gaze so intense. I could tell he wanted me as much as I didn't want to want him. Not if he wasn't going to be honest.

I picked up my purse and followed Renn outside, hoping he'd be more talkative out in the open.

But he simply stood there, staring at me, looking as if he had something to say. An awkward silence inched between us.

"See you soon, Jessica." He ran the back of his finger down my cheek.

With my hand against the spot he had just touched, I watched him walk away, waiting to see him shimmer, or waver, or for anything odd. But nothing happened.

He crossed the street and kept on walking. I wanted to follow him with every fiber in my body.

Go then. My heart screamed at me. I took a few steps in his direction, willing him to turn around and glance at me. All I needed was one look and I would have started running toward him.

Destined-to-be-lovers are always glancing at each other in the movies. He stopped. Yes! He was sure to turn around.

"Hey Jess." Nola poked her head out the door. "Can you give me hand with something."

I looked at her for one split second. When I turned back around, Renn was gone.

Chapter Six

Renn traveled by taxi to his motel room in Malibu.
Why Central Match had booked him a room so far from
Jessica's home was beyond him. There weren't any
rules about where a traveler had to stay when on his
mission. Staying within walking distance would have
been preferable.

Riding in the backseat of a car did not fit his fragile
physical state. For the second time since his arrival he
found himself getting dizzy as the driver, a guy in his
thirties with a buzz cut, took the canyon curves too
sharply.

Time traveling would have been quicker and
easier. Arlianna had advised against it and, considering
what had happened earlier, he knew he needed to
adhere to her rules.

Renn prepared himself, should the car swerve off
the cliff. In which case, he'd be forced to teleport,
leaving the crazy-ass driver to fend for himself.

To keep himself sane, he thought about how
Jessica's smile made every nerve in his body come
alive. Until he remembered her smile was meant for
Frank Griffin. Then he felt his blood pressure climb.
Better to watch the mountains and keep breathing
deeply.

After one particularly sharp curve, the driver
looked into the rear-view mirror and asked Renn how

his night was going.

"It's going," he answered, tucking his thumbs inside his fists.

His driver let out a long chuckle. "That's for sure."

"Nothing is for sure," Renn disagreed.

"Well, that's for sure."

Renn couldn't wait to get out of this car. The driver made a few more ridiculous statements as they cruised down the Pacific Coast Highway.

"Ocean looks calm tonight."

Did that call for an answer?

"The stars look crowded. Don't ya say?"

Another inane statement.

As they pulled up to the motel, the meter stopped at eighty-six dollars. Renn took a hundred-dollar bill from his wallet, handed it to the driver, and told him to keep the change.

"Thanks, buddy," the driver said. "They serve a great corned beef hash at Bettys, just up a ways. Take care."

Renn shut the taxi door. He could care less about hash or the moon or anything at the moment. He wanted the evening to pass into daylight.

Once inside his motel room, he pulled out his tablet and began his report.

From the log of Renn Porter, Apprentice Matchmaker

Mentor: Arlianna Greenhouse

Mission# 265 – Griffin & Singleton

Day Two PM – Final Report

Something is off.

Can't complete data at this time.

Add'l Notes:

Lost CORE. 100% detachment. Experienced a time jerk.

Looking into flaws.

Submitted: Neg

He couldn't send the data even though he knew it was mandatory. His action put Arlianna at risk, too, since he was her apprentice. She stood behind him, believed in him.

If Arlianna put her stamp of approval on his findings, they wouldn't have to transport Jessica. But this was his first assignment. Going against Central Match could get him fired. Maybe his judgement was clouded by all the pulls in time he'd been experiencing.

Still. He couldn't, and he wouldn't send his report. Not today.

Instead, he sent another PM to his mentor, hoping she would delete it immediately and provide him with the answer he needed.

Mission #265

Confidential Memo

To: Arlianna Greenhouse

From: Renn Porter

I am 100% certain of flaws. Not the right match. Need more time. Please advise.

Chapter Seven

I woke up at two-thirty in the morning, my heart pounding, remembering the details of my dream as they slipped away. Renn and I strolled through a dense forest to a clearing. We sat on a bench, holding hands. The scene cut jarringly to a beach. A tidal wave rose and barreled toward us. Renn grabbed me, pressing his lips on mine.

I could still feel his kiss, firm yet inviting.

Rolling over, I fell back into another dream. This time we sped down a mountain on a large piece of cardboard. A gigantic boulder loomed in front of us. Seconds before crashing, Renn kissed me again.

When I next opened my eyes, I was drenched in sweat, feeling disoriented. The familiar glowing green of the clock showed the time at six-thirty. My shift didn't start until ten o'clock, but rather than fall back into another dream, I got up.

I did a few yoga stretches, showered, and left for work.

Before leaving the break room, I took the piece of material out of my purse. It was bone cold, like dry ice, and stuck to my fingers, so that I had to peel it off to get it into my apron pocket.

For some unexplainable reason, I had to have it near me. Not that anyone ever stole things from the break room, but it was the only thing I cared about from my purse. Everything else was replaceable.

I texted Lilly to call me the minute her plane arrived, tucked my purse into my cubby, and went onto the floor.

I relieved Ashley at the register and instructed her to straighten up the condiment bar.

Since there were no customers, I decided to get myself a cup of coffee, the only thing we're allowed to drink on the house.

"Excuse me."

I turned around to face a woman about my aunt's age with tons of curly blonde hair. A jolt of energy ran through my body. Even though I had only seen her from the back the other day, I knew it was the woman that had been walking with Renn.

Her trench coat hung open exposing a simple white blouse with large gold buttons, way too gaudy. They didn't seem to fit with her plain face or her kind eyes, which seemed to recognize me.

"What can I get you?" I asked.

"Two small nonfat lattes, hold the foam, please." Her melodic voice made me smile.

"Anything else?" I asked, wondering who had accompanied her. "Some pastry or a muffin?"

"No, thank you." Her words drifted toward me on waves.

"Your name?"

"Arlianna."

I scribbled her name on the cups and set them down for Ashley, feeling Arlianna's eyes on me the whole time.

"That's six forty-five."

She handed me a ten-dollar bill, smiled, and then

looked over her shoulder. Something in the way she strained her neck, or the sudden tightness of her lips made me bite on the inside of my cheek.

Following her gaze, my eyes landed on the outside patio. The strange woman from the pharmacy sat at a table. Her pencil thin lips pressed together. Although there was a dozen customers and the large glass window between us, I could feel her anger barreling toward me. Which made no sense. I didn't even know her. But I knew she didn't like me. What I didn't understand was why.

Her pencil thin lips pressed together. Although there was a dozen customers and the large glass window between us, I could feel her anger barreling toward me. Which made no sense. I didn't even know her. But I knew she didn't like me. What I didn't understand was why.

When Arlianna turned back toward me, I noticed the tiny tattoo on her earlobe. It was both a flower and heart depending on how she moved her head. It was amazingly beautiful, and so strange that I stood there clutching her money.

"Miss?" Arlianna held out her hand. "My change, please."

"Of course." With sweaty palms, I managed to hand Arlianna her money. Once she left the coffeeshop, I told Ashley to cover the register while I took a break.

By the time I got outside, the women were halfway down the block. My spirit sank, all hope of catching them deflated. I turned and went back to work.

While I was getting a simple drip for a jogger, my pocket began to grow warm. Two lattes latter, the heat grew almost unbearable.

This was not my imagination.

While making change, I saw Renn outside. He leaned up against a pole, arms crossed. The drink slipped from my hand, landing sideways on the counter.

"Sorry," I mumbled. "It's on me."

I started to leave when the next customer, a man in a suit, asked for a decaf drip. Hurriedly, I poured him one, took his money, and was getting ready to go when the next customer started talking to me.

This guy was a mind-mess as Kyle calls the ones who can't make up their mind in less than a minute. Latte or cappuccino? Mocha or vanilla? One shot, two shots.

"What's in an Americano?" the customer asked.

"It's got… Ashley, take over." I walked away from the customer who had now moved onto questions about our blended drinks.

I lifted up the counter separating the work area from the floor and let myself out. Just as I reached the exit, Nancy, a friend of my aunt's, barged through the entrance. She smelled like garlic and talked in that rushed way of hers, as if someone had pushed her fast forward button.

"Jessie. I didn't expect you here this late? How are your grandparents? Your aunt? What's going on with everyone? I haven't seen your aunt in ages."

"Fine. Everyone's good," I said, bouncing on the balls of my feet, keeping my eyes on Renn.

"Are you on your break?" Nancy asked. "Come sit with me, so I can catch up."

I moved so that I could see outside the glass door. Renn wiped off one of the chairs and sat down.

"I have to go, Nancy." I tried to move around her.

I couldn't leave without a hug. Once I was free, I rushed outside. Renn watched as I walked toward him.

"Hey." I smiled. Heat radiated from my pocket.

"Hey." He motioned for me to sit.

I sat across from him. "Your friend was just in here getting coffee."

He looked down at the table.

"The lady I saw you walking with, when I thought I saw you, that is."

"Don't believe everything you see," he said. "It's a bad habit."

He steadied his eyes on mine, making me doubt I had seen them walking the other night. His lips turned upward at the corners.

"You want a latte?" I asked. "On me."

"On you?" He raised his eyebrows slightly. "That sounds inviting."

A slow heat crept into my cheeks. My skin tingled. "It could be the best invitation you'll get all week." I couldn't believe that suggestion came out of my mouth.

"I don't doubt it."

A homeless man shuffled toward us. "Can you spare some change?" The man held out his hand. Dirty fingers poked through the tips of his worn glove.

I reached into my pocket for some quarters, touching the fabric from Renn's coat.

The air ripped around me. A sharp pain started in my toes and traveled up my body. My head throbbed. My chair rocked backward. To keep from falling, I grabbed onto the table, my knuckles white from exertion.

Regaining my balance, I looked up. Renn was gone.

The homeless man shuffled toward me. He held out his hand, just as he had a few seconds ago. "Can you spare some change?"

****

The sand, the music, the salty air. It was familiar. But why here, in this time and place again? Renn was baffled beyond comprehension.

He moved slowly toward the party, the sound of the waves crashing into his confusion. His shoes sank into the sand. With each step, his body fell lower into the earth until he was sure his legs were knee deep into the ground. But no. When he looked down, he could still see the tops of his shoes.

His locator lit up. Arlianna sent an onslaught of emojis. Not one of them was smiling.

He answered immediately.

Mission #265

Instant Communication

Renn: Booted again!

Arlianna: Same time?

Renn: Affirm. Same wedding. Dancing. Whitney Houston singing "I want to dance with somebody who loves me."

Arlianna: Meet me @ home base I have info

Renn: Why is this occurring?

Arlianna: I have my suspicions

Meet her at home base? How the hell was he supposed to get there?

Chapter Eight

The Future

Natasha Aftergood twirled the old-fashioned pencil, a number 2, between her thumb and forefinger, watching the monitor on her desk.

Two of her best matchmakers were completing their missions. Their final logs came in within seconds of each other.

She allowed herself a slight smile, before speaking into her holocom. "Lexi, has Renn Porter completed his report?"

Lexi's round face materialized in front of her. "No, ma'am."

"Have you heard from him today?"

"No, ma'am, not a peep."

Natasha pushed on the pencil with her thumbs until it started to crack. What a fool that Arlianna was. Letting her apprentice run with the mission.

"Shall I try to make contact?" Lexi asked.

"No. I'll take care of it myself."

Natasha rolled her finger over the holocom, watching as Lexi's face disappeared. She stared into the blank space, anger sizzling inside her like hot oil.

This was not how she had planned on spending the next few days. She had wanted to get a new Tatt. Now that she had successfully signed off on her one thousandth match, she was eligible for an upgrade.

Something smaller, more delicate.

One thousand matches. Natasha thought back to that first one. How different life had been.

She hadn't always been driven by money. When she had first been promoted to president after having proven herself as a skilled matchmaker, she had vowed to review every single mission and make sure that all her Travelers followed every single law.

But over the years things had changed.

At first it had been a small incident. The customer had been insistent Natasha find his soulmate. He had beaucoup debits, offering to pay well over the stated price. It was hard to refuse him. She had found someone raised in foster care. A young woman who had been shuffled from home to home, eventually ending up in trouble with the law. Natasha reasoned the girl deserved a better life. It was a one-time situation, a win-win match. No one would ever be the wiser.

But it had been so easy that the next time when she knew there wasn't a soul mate for that wealthy Robotics guy, she altered the data just a nano sec and found someone for him.

Ditto on the next two matches. No one ever complained.

At the annual meeting, the board had praised her for raising the profits by 15% over the previous year and given her a substantial bonus. And who could refuse that? No one in their right orbit would turn down that kind of cash especially with a gallon of milk costing over seven debits.

After that it became second nature. A little shift here. A delete there. And no one suspected a thing. Until now. Now that little blip of an apprentice was getting in her orbit.

Well, not if Natasha had anything to say about the matter. And if Seth found out. Well, she didn't even want to speculate on that data. Besides, he loved the debits she was bringing in.

Natasha turned on her O-Book, scrolled down to *The Handbook* and read through the laws. Many of them had been written by herself.

She stopped at **Law #99 – "The final decision to take the subject through time rests in the hands of the Matchmaker. He must be 100% certain in the direction he chooses."**

Why had she ever approved this law?

It left little room for interpretation. Shutting off the O-Book she muttered, "In order to complete this mission the matchmaker must be deleted. In this case, that's you, Renn."

That little blip surely didn't know the power of who he was up against.

Chapter Nine

I poured shots of espresso. *Time does not repeat.* I heated milk. *Time does not repeat.* I wiped the wands. *Time does not repeat.* The phrase became my mantra for the afternoon. A never-ending loop, weaving between the customers' voices, the scrape of chairs moving across the floor, the dings, and chimes of cell phones. Time does not repeat. Said enough times, I hoped I could believe myself.

But time did repeat itself. That little girl did tie her shoes twice. The homeless man did shuffle toward me more than once.

I couldn't get past what I had witnessed. Either time had repeated itself, or I was losing my mind.

Kyle started his shift at 4:30. At 5:00 the usual rush began. I switched from the bar station to the register where I proceeded to screw up one drink after another.

"What's wrong with you today?" Kyle asked after I'd X'd the wrong box on the cup for the third time.

"Nothing." Everything.

Ashley kept asking me to write legibly so she could actually read the orders.

"It's a Decaf Double Shot Non Fat Latte Extra hot. See." But she had a point. I was having trouble reading my own scribbles.

"Okay." Ashley pressed her trembling lips together.

Fuck. She was going to cry.

"Sorry, Ash," I said. "Do you want to switch? I'll work the bar with Kyle."

"No." Her bottom lip trembled.

"Hang in there. It gets easier."

Finally, things slowed, and I went outside for my fifteen-minute break.

"You got a minute, Jess?" Kyle asked sitting down next to me.

"You left her in there alone?" I nodded toward Ashley.

"She'll be fine."

I doubted she'd be fine, but I didn't have enough energy to worry about Ashley at the moment.

Kyle laced his fingers together and cracked his knuckles, his big eyes getting even larger. "Any more contact with Renn?"

"Nope," I lied, unconvincingly.

"I know you too well, Jess. You can't lie to me."

"Then why ask?"

Two women, each pushing a stroller, stopped outside The Hut. The taller one opened the door, struggling to get her stroller through the entrance. Kyle got up and helped them maneuver inside.

Without thinking, I reached in my pocket for the fabric and pulled it out. It was cold again, just as icy as it had been earlier this morning. I wondered what made it change temperature. I saw Kyle watching me as he walked back to our table and quickly tucked it inside my pocket.

"Watch yourself around him. He's got something weird going on."

"He could use some life-coaching advice," I teased.

"About the proper way to say goodbye."

"I wish you'd take me seriously. And by the way, I have two clients now."

"That's great," I said. I really did want Kyle's life coaching business to succeed. "And I will be careful. Don't worry." I nodded my head toward the entrance. "We should get back inside."

"In a minute. Say, Jess." Kyle moved his chair closer to mine. "I do have something I have to tell you. I had it out with Heather this morning. I told her it was over. O.V.E.R, over."

He reached for my hand, but then pulled back. I knew he wanted to touch me and joke about his magnetism. We'd been there. Done that. And since meeting Renn, I knew for certain Kyle and I were meant to stay friends.

"But you guys are so good together," I said, trying to put some sense into him. "Who else likes those mayo and peanut butter sandwiches?"

"You."

"Once. I ate it once because you made me."

Kyle cracked his knuckles again.

"You'll find someone," I said. "And you'll know it when you do. We better get back to work."

The last hour of my shift dragged on. Six o'clock couldn't come fast enough. Every time I checked my phone, it was only a minute later. Time was not only repeating itself, it seemed to be standing still.

Chapter Ten

After work, I spent a half hour chatting with my grandparents. Actually, listening more than talking. I tracked Lilly's flight on my phone and excused myself when I saw the plane had landed.

—See you on the porch.—

Lilly's text lifted my spirits like nothing else could. I poured a glass of wine and went to their porch to wait.

Sitting there brought back a million memories.

Throughout the years we talked about everything from the right way to put in a tampon, to the benefits of not having a boyfriend, to her wishing she wasn't a year ahead of me in school, but never about anything as strange as what was now happening.

I couldn't sit still. The anticipation of finally seeing Lilly unleashed a flood of energy inside me. By the time she pulled into the driveway, I'd walked at least a mile up and down her driveway.

After hugging for about a minute, Lilly and I looked at each other and then we hugged again.

"You look fantastic," I said at the same time she was telling me how good I looked. But I wasn't lying. She did look terrific.

Her blonde hair fell in waves to her shoulders. Even after a twelve-hour plane ride, it wasn't matted or flattened like mine would have been.

She had on brown yoga pants with a tight tank top

and sandals that strapped around her ankles about five times. Not dressed at all like the jeans and sweatshirt Lilly who had left for London a year ago.

"How about these clothes?" she asked, twirling around. "You were right, Jess. I did need a change."

"Well, you look awesome."

She'd lost about ten pounds and gained about fifty degrees of happiness.

"And I love your new glasses," I said.

"Black looks good, don't you think? I got tired of those wire ones."

Her mom popped open the trunk and lifted out a huge suitcase.

"Oh, my God," she said, dropping the bag onto the driveway. "Did you pack everything you own?"

"I thought you were lifting weights now, Mom." Lilly picked up her suitcase.

"Not ones this heavy." Her mom laughed, kissing Lilly on the cheek. If I hadn't been watching them all my life, this would have made me sad, ache even more for my mother. As it was, I felt a tiny ping. But my happiness in seeing Lilly left no room for sorrow to creep in.

I took Lilly's laptop from the backseat and followed her into her house, up the familiar stairs, and into her old room.

After she moved to London, Lilly's parents replaced the beige carpeting with hardwood floors, and painted the walls a soft blue. They kept her photographs on the walls, mostly portraits. The gigantic throw pillows she loved still covered her bed.

Being in this room reminded me it had been over five years since our days at college. Over a year since

Lilly finally moved out and gone to London. Here I was, still with my grandparents. Lilly was going places, whereas I seemed to be going nowhere, but insane.

Lilly lit one of the candles her mom had placed on the dresser, making it even more like it used to be. The vanilla scent came at me, opening a door to a million memories.

I didn't even know I was crying until Lilly handed me a tissue. She sat down next to me, wrapping her arm around my shoulders. She was so much like her mother, comforting in a quiet way. I wondered if I was like mine.

"I'm losing my mind," I finally said, when the tears had stopped.

"You are not." Lilly squeezed my hand. "There has to be a logical explanation for what's going on."

"Well, if there is, I hope you can find it." I sat up and pulled the fabric from my pocket.

"It's kind of silky," she said, petting it like a puppy. "But different. It feels cold, almost wet."

"It heats up when Renn gets close to me," I said, taking it back from her. "It was flaming hot when he disappeared. And then time moved backward and repeated itself. Exactly the same way."

"That's something to go by. A big something, if you ask me." She lugged her suitcase to the bed. "It's possible the material changes the lighting around you. Or maybe it has some kind of hypnotizing thing about it. Making you think you see him disappear and time repeats, but he's really there all along," Lilly said.

"And that's normal?" I flopped onto her bed, hugging an oversized pillow to my chest.

"Well, no." She bit on the side of her lip, smiling.

A smile I didn't realize how much I had missed.

"One minute I think none of this could be happening, and then the next I know it is," I said. "And the strangest part of all is I know there is something between us. Something physical happens. Not just an excitement like with David at the beginning. This is so much more intense."

"We're going to get to the bottom of all this."

She sounded so cheerful and positive, I started to think we'd figure it all out.

She opened up her suitcase, releasing a ton of sweaters, shirts, jeans, and dresses. Tucked in the corners were five pairs of shoes and two pairs of boots. "No wonder that thing is so heavy." I picked up a pair of five-inch red heels and dangled them in front of her. "Going somewhere I don't know about?"

"It's hard to pack not knowing what I'll be doing."

"Looks like you have something planned."

Lilly gave me her half smile, snatching the shoes out of my hand. "They're for the wedding."

"Right."

"Well, what if we go out?" She set the shoes in her closet. "Maybe Renn has a single friend."

"Not so fast," I said. "Let's figure him out first."

She lined bottles of lotions and creams on her dresser. Put the last of her underwear in the drawer and shoved the suitcase into the closet. "Do you work tomorrow?"

"No. I'm off. But…" I said, pressing on my cheek with my thumb.

"But you're going?" Lilly raised her eyebrows.

I nodded.

"Then I'm going with."

She stretched out on her bed, yawning.

I left a few hours later, promising not to go to The Hut without her.

If only I had kept that promise.

Chapter Eleven

The next day, I woke up with the sunrise. From my bed, I watched my tree change from a dark silhouette against the pink sky into a green leafy magnificence.

I found comfort in her faithfulness. If I ever did move, I'd miss her terribly.

Her branches seemed to speak to me, and I agreed with her advice. It was time to write again.

I slipped my hand under my pillow. For a split second I thought the fabric from Renn's coat had disappeared, but then my fingers touched its cold, silky texture. Relieved, I picked it up and tucked it into my pajama pocket.

Time to get to work.

I dusted off the cover of my journal and turned to the last entry written months ago.

David's a shit. I'm better off without him. I hadn't believed those words at the time, but I did now. Looking back, I'd wasted too much energy on him, making sure he was always happy. My writing had stalled. My motivation had stalled. My entire life had stalled.

I flipped to a clean page and started writing…

Every time the mysterious man drew closer to the woman, he disappeared, as if he defied the laws of gravity. Her world shifted. She craved to know more. Her entire being depended on it.

The words poured out of me, marching across the blank page like soldiers lined up for action. By the time I stopped, they covered three pages and the sun was shining through my blinds, warm and inviting.

I opened the door leading to my tiny porch and greeted my tree with a wave. Her branches arched toward me. "Thanks," I whispered. As I turned around, a leaf drifted to my arm. I held it for a second, admiring its perfect symmetry. And then I set it free.

Not up to making coffee, I walked through my apartment and into the main house for a cup.

A postcard sat on the kitchen table. It was picture of wild-maned horses running across a field. I turned it over. "Hey Honey Pie. How are you? Life is good here. Filming in Arezzo tomorrow. Xoxoxoxox Pa."

"Good morning."

I jumped, dropping the postcard.

"Oh, sweetie, I didn't mean to scare you," Grandma said. "You're up early."

"Sounds like he's having fun." I picked up the card. "I wonder what it's like for him, filming in the town where he met Mom."

"Bittersweet, probably."

"I really miss him."

"I know you do," Grandma said, rubbing my arm. "He should be home soon."

And then gone again. But that was his life. My father, the wanderer. Maybe the next time he came home he would stay longer than his usual two weeks. Probably not.

"There should be enough in the coffee maker." Grandma motioned to the pot. "I'm going to jump into the shower."

I poured myself a cup and carried it to my apartment to get dressed.

My phone was playing its wake-up song. I turned it off and then texted Lilly. When she didn't answer, I called and left a message.

Ten minutes later, with the fabric tucked in the tiny pocket of my tank top, I was ready to leave.

Jet lag must have gotten to Lilly. I thought of banging on her front door but then she'd be a grumpy mess half the day. Instead, I texted telling her to meet me at The Hut.

The place was packed, a normal nine o'clock morning. An elderly couple sat at Renn's usual table. I scanned the place, although I didn't see or feel him anywhere.

Ashley worked the bar while Nola rang up the sales.

"Hey, Jess," Ashley said. "Aren't you off today?"

"I'm meeting a friend here. Ash, I'm sorry about yesterday."

"No worries," she said. "You want a latte?"

I really didn't need any more caffeine, but Ashley seemed eager to make me one. I didn't want to hurt her feelings again.

Taking the latte, I found some shade in front of the ice cream parlor next door and leaned up against the wall to people watch. Deep inside of me, my creative juices bubbled, just as they had earlier this morning.

A tall, wiry guy walked by.

"Hey, Jess." He nodded. He lives on my block and knows my name, probably from seeing me at work. But if I ever knew his name, I didn't know it now.

I waved at him and watched as he sat down with a

bunch of guys. They were all younger than me, about college age, and I started wondering about their lives. If maybe the guy with the gold earring was good in math or if the one with the thick glasses spent a lot of time playing video games.

When my phone sang out, I almost dropped it.

"You promised not to go without me," Lilly said. "Are you still at The Hut?"

"I'm outside people watching."

"I'll be there in fifteen."

I went back to my stories, going around the table of guys, feeling good that my brain was once again working like it used to. I was giving the guy with the earring a red-haired, passionate girlfriend when a pinprick of heat shot through my side.

My hands shook as I texted Lilly. —*He's here.*—

—*On my way*—

I stuck my finger into my tiny pocket. The fabric was warm and getting hotter as I rubbed it. I looked everywhere.

A young mom pushed a stroller. An older lady sat reading a book. Two little girls argued over a straw.

I scanned the parking lot, my heart thudding hard and fast. If my theory was right, Renn should appear within seconds.

The door of the yogurt shop opened. A woman in a sundress came out and there he was, right behind her.

Our eyes met, and a fire burned between us. He smiled, moving his chin up slightly. My heart accelerated against my chest like a speeding train.

I moved toward him.

Out of nowhere, Arlianna's friend, the woman from the pharmacy materialized a few feet behind

Renn. As if she came from the air, pulling the molecules together to form her being. She walked quickly, shortening the distance between them.

"Turn around," I shouted.

He kept moving forward. The strange woman closed the gap between them.

"Watch out!" I shouted louder.

Her eyes caught mine. In that instant, I knew it wasn't Renn who was in danger.

She shoved him out of the way and came toward me. With the fabric in my hand, I turned around and started running. I reached the parking lot when a blast of wind pushed me backward.

The air ripped around me. Fiercer than ever before. I hunched my shoulders, clutching at my sides, as the pain cut through me. The ground moved sideways.

I took a few steps forward, reaching for something, a parked car or a post, anything to get my balance.

Suddenly there was her twisted face, grabbing my hand. Everything moved fast forward. I saw images, things I know that had not happened to me. Not yet. My hands holding a film clapboard. My hand with a ring on it that I'd never seen before. With a jolt, the reel shifted and started going backward. Images of my past zoomed before my eyes. Mom singing at the kitchen sink. My father carrying a bouquet of red roses.

With another jolt, the images stopped long enough for me to see the woman, grinning at me. Her coat fanned around her body, like a fireworks display. She let go of my hand. Everything went white.

****

Renn stood helpless as Natasha had her way with Jessica. Her powers outstretched his. He concentrated on his CORE, but he slammed into a brick wall. Immovable, unpassable.

Jessica's scream pierced the air, circling around him. And then she was gone.

And he was…where? Where was he?

Mission #265

Instant Communication

Renn: U were right N got her

Arlianna: DNP Get back here

Renn: OMG ?????

Arlianna: Repeat…Do Not Panic

Chapter Twelve

What is going on? Why is there an IV in my arm? Everyone is looking at me like I'm dying. Why are they standing so still?

Aunt Beth. Grandma. Grandpa. Lilly. Kyle. Each one stood inside their own picture frame. They needed to be spliced together.

In unison, their heads turned away from me and toward the door. I looked to see what they were looking at. I heard footsteps. A split second later, a tall female in a white coat entered the room.

She introduced herself to my family. Her squeaky voice grated against my skin. I only heard the word doctor. She held herself upright, authority written all over her posture. I disliked her immediately.

Everyone moved forward, slowly. But at least they were moving and merging together.

My aunt's mouth opened. I didn't hear anything. Not at first. Her lips moved. Seconds later her voice followed. "Can she hear us?"

My eyes moved to the doctor as she adjusted the machine at my side. Her mouth opened, too, without any words. As it closed, I heard her voice. "Possibly."

Kyle's mouth opened and then Lilly's and Aunt Beth's, and trying to follow the sentences overlapping each other made me nauseous. They bombarded the doctor with the same questions.

"Please," Grandma said, moving toward the bed. The mattress shifted underneath me a few seconds after she sat down on the side. "Everyone please, not so loud."

I saw my hand moving up. Seconds later I saw Grandma's wrinkled hand on my skin.

What is happening to me?

I stared into my grandmother's eyes. They are light blue, soft and powdery. Today, they looked exceptionally beautiful, even though I could tell she'd been crying.

"Can you hear me?" she asked, her lips and words still out of sync.

I can hear you, Grandma. I tried to transmit those words to her.

With all the other weirdness going on, maybe I could.

She kept staring at me, rubbing my hand. When she clasped her hands together, I continued to feel her fingers on my skin.

The doctor lowered her face close to mine. I read her nametag, Doctor Victoria Lawrence. I smelled peppermint as she shined a bright light into my eyes. I thought for sure I blinked, but no one seemed to notice, so I must not have.

Scream! I told my brain.

Nothing.

But I know I'm moving my fingers. I can feel it. Why can't anyone see that?

"Is she in a coma?" Lilly asked, brushing the hair off my face. I felt her fingertips as she raised her hand.

"Not exactly." Dr. Lawrence typed something into the computer in the corner of the room. "Her pupils are responding. Her vitals are fine. A little low. There's no sign of brain damage. Her heartbeat is steady but…" She paused, her nostrils flaring.

"But what?" Aunt Beth jumped into the space created by the doctor's sigh.

The doctor shook her head. "But…unusually slow. It's as if any second she should revive, but…well I really can't explain it."

Oh God. What's happening? I'm here. But not here. Like in between time. I'm dying! My heart is about to explode!

I stared at my hand. The last thing I remembered was that horrible woman touching it.

That's it. I'm going to vanish, just like Renn had! What if I don't come back?

"I've never seen a case like this." The doctor got up from the computer and stood at the foot of my bed.

"Well, I know what's wrong." Kyle's big eyes filled with anger. "She's been drugged. God damn it, and I know that freak did it to her."

"Drugs!" Lilly sneered at Kyle. "Jess doesn't do drugs."

"No, but I bet that Renn guy slipped her something."

"You're crazy," Lilly argued.

My eardrums vibrated from their loud voices.

"Lilly, Kyle please be quiet," Aunt Beth said. "Let the doctor talk. She's trying to say something."

Doctor Lawrence rubbed the side of her nose with her ring finger. Sparkles shot off her diamond ring. "It's not drugs. Her tox screen came back clean."

"Then what the hell is wrong with her?" Kyle gripped the railing at the edge of the bed. His energy vibrated beneath me.

"It's like she's in pause mode or something," Lilly said. I could imagine her brain cells churning away, searching for an explanation.

The doctor rubbed her nose again. "Hmmm…Interesting. You could call it that."

Interesting! My life is hanging over a cliff, and she calls it interesting!

"Then push the damn play button." Kyle paced the room.

Aunt Beth sniffed. It sounded like someone cutting through plastic. Grandpa's snores blasted from the corner of the room.

"Let's see how she is in a few hours." The doctor's smile reminded me of weak coffee. I was glad to see her leave.

"I know he did something to her," Kyle said. "Maybe not drugs, but something. She thinks he disappears, Lilly. Tell me that's normal."

"Will someone please tell me what is going on?" Grandma said, keeping her eyes on mine.

I'm sorry I didn't tell you about him.

"Some weirdo who's been stalking her." Kyle stopped in front of the window. The sunlight cast a halo around his head.

"He's not a stalker," Lilly said.

"And you know this how?" Kyle asked. "You haven't even seen him."

"Jess told me about him." Lilly glanced at me. "She said he was different, in a good way. She likes him."

"Will someone please tell me what you're all talking about," Grandma pleaded, her eyes still on mine.

"What do you mean, disappears?" Grandpa asked, out of nowhere.

"Jess thinks this guy she met becomes invisible." Kyle looked at my grandfather. "She's hallucinating, what else could it be?"

Lilly spoke directly to my aunt. "Jess is not a liar. You know that. We all know that."

You tell them, Lilly. I'm not. I may be crazy, but I'm not a liar.

Tears pushed against my eyes.

So much pressure. Why can't I cry?

"Are you talking about the guy she met at work?" Aunt Beth sat down at the foot of my bed. The mattress sagged several seconds after she sat down.

Lilly nodded.

"Renn was there when she passed out," Kyle said. "Obviously, he's involved."

"I said Jess said he was coming." Lilly pointed a finger at Kyle. "Not that he was there."

"Did he call her?" Kyle asked.

"Not exactly," Lilly said, looking into my eyes.

"What then?"

"That piece of material warms up when he's nearby."

"Now I've heard everything. Where is it?" Kyle walked up to Lilly. "I'm having it analyzed. Maybe it's laced with LSD or some type of designer drug. I know she takes it with her everywhere."

NO! Please, Lilly, don't let him take it from me.

"She has been acting strange lately," Grandma said.

"What's going on?" Grandpa asked. "Can I have

something to drink?"

Grandma pressed her lips together. I heard them smack a second later as she lifted up the water pitcher and filled up a paper cup. The water sounded like music as it poured out of the pitcher.

I must be dying. That's it. No one ever comes back to tell us what it's like. This could be it. This is death.

I heard Grandpa's heavy breathing as Grandma handed him the water.

"Where's the material?" Kyle asked.

NO. Don't take it from me.

"Lilly, do you know where it is?" Aunt Beth asked. "I think Kyle's right. If it came from that guy, we should have it checked out."

"Where are you going to take it?" Lilly asked.

"My cousin works for a forensics lab."

NO! Without the fabric, I could be like this forever.

"It should be in the pocket of whatever she was wearing when they brought her in here. I'm sorry, Jess." Lilly kissed me on the cheek. I felt her lips as she started talking again. "I love you, you know that. But seeing you like this is horrible."

Everything is so off, out of sync. My head hurts so much.

"By all means, we have to find this person," my grandfather said.

Kyle opened the closet. He pulled my clothes out of the plastic bag.

Lilly didn't say anything. She played with her hair as Kyle searched through my pockets until he found the material.

"Got it." He held it in his hands. "This thing is cold and slimy."

Please. No. Those words screamed inside me, tumbled around like inside a bottle, unable to find the way out.

"Call me if anything changes." With the fabric in his hand, Kyle left the room.

"I'm going with him." Lilly gave me a quick kiss and rushed after Kyle.

I felt better knowing that Lilly was going along, but I felt far from complete.

Help me.

I stared into my grandmother's eyes. A tear rolled down her cheek and landed on my arm. A split second later the wetness crept into my skin.

Please, help me.

Chapter Thirteen

With Lilly and Kyle gone, the room grew quiet except for the sounds of my family breathing. Inhales and exhales crisscrossed the air, like freeway overpasses. I huddled beneath them, mesmerized by the sounds.

Short, shallow breaths came from my grandmother. Aunt Beth took longer, deeper inhales and let them out slowly. Grandpa's breathing held a wheezy sound.

As strange as these sounds were, I found them fascinating and comforting.

I'm not sure how long this went on. Time didn't seem to make any sense. It could have been an hour or maybe only a few minutes when my aunt suggested she and Grandma get something to eat.

Aunt Beth's lips moved. A second later, her words reached me. "We'll be right back, Daddy. You stay here with Jessie."

Grandma sighed, but she agreed with Aunt Beth. Before leaving, she kissed me on the lips. As her face moved away from mine, I tasted salt.

Aunt Beth kissed me on the cheek. "I love you."

I read her lips, knowing the words would follow.

I love you.

Now the only breathing was that of my grandfather. A cloudy inhale and exhale. I wished he could breathe easier.

I'm sorry if I haven't always been so nice to you.

As if he heard me, Grandpa opened his eyes and smiled at me. Pushing on the table for balance he managed to get out of the chair and using his cane walked slowly to the side of my bed. He looked down at me. "I don't know what's wrong with you, honey. But the doctors will figure it out." He squeezed my hand. His fingers were cold. "Don't worry." It was the same as with my aunt. His lips moved. I heard his words a second later.

Okay, Grandpa. I hope you're right.

He shuffled back to the chair and within minutes, thunderous snores cut through his uneven breathing, one about every five seconds.

I counted to four, ready for another loud snort, when I heard a rustling at the door. It sounded like papers crinkling. I didn't see anything for several seconds, or maybe longer. The air swirled like a swarm of bees. And her face appeared. That horrible woman who had paralyzed me like this.

My heart pounded against my chest like a fist.

"Hello Jessica," her voice sounded like nails on glass.

Oh, my God. What is she doing here? Grandpa, wake up! Please.

I thrashed my legs against the mattress. I tossed my head back and forth. I thought I was moving, but my grandfather didn't notice a thing.

The woman who had done this to me moved closer. Daggered sparkles shot off the surface of her coat, heading in my direction.

Grandpa! Someone. Anyone.

An earth-shattering snore tore through the room.

Her lips twisted into her evil smile. When she reached the side of my bed, she leaned down. Her breath was black, pungent smelling. Sucking the life out of me.

Help.

I squeezed my eyes shut, tightening my muscles. Or maybe I didn't move at all.

Get away. Leave me alone.

"Jessie?"

The woman turned away from me and toward my grandfather. His breathing quickened. He jabbed his cane at her. A useless effort. All she did was cackle.

I couldn't see the woman's face, but my grandfather's wide eyes and trembling lips told me everything.

Run, Grandpa!

My grandfather shrunk back in his chair. He seemed small, engulfed by the dark energy swirling through the room.

"Natasha, leave him alone!"

Renn's lemony scent floated toward me. It settled upon me like a warm bath, bubbling against my skin. He appeared a second later.

The woman lifted her arm in the air. "You!"

The room tumbled. I was falling...falling... A sudden jerk and everything settled.

Grandpa sat in the chair, grinning at me. Natasha was gone.

Renn's trench coat shimmered as he moved to my side. My heart jumped up and down.

I flinched when he sat on the edge of the bed. I couldn't help myself.

"Jessica." His mouth moved in sync with my name.

Everything about him was in sync. His lips matched his touch, his smell, his eyes, his smile, his skin.

I stared into his amazing eyes, mesmerized by the contrast between the blue center and dark rim.

"It's over." His voice came at me like a lullaby. "Don't worry."

I wanted to believe him. But I still couldn't move.

Don't let go of my hand.

And then before I realized what was happening, he bent over and pressed his lips against mine. His tongue was warm and searching. Every nerve in my body responded to his kiss. Every muscle, every fiber awoke to this new sensation. His soft bristles brushed gently against my skin. At the moment, nothing else in the world mattered.

When the kiss was over, our eyes held onto each other for what seemed like a full-length feature movie. Everything in the room was right again. I lifted my hand in the air, turned it back and forth. I kicked my legs.

"Can you hear me?" I asked.

"Every word," he said, making no attempt to wipe the tear running down his face.

"And you can see me moving? I am moving?"

"You are." He nodded.

"What happened to me?" I reached up and touched his hair. Its silkiness fell through my fingers. "What did that woman do to me? It was like I was in a coma. But I could hear and see everything."

"Too much 411 to explain right now," he said, taking my hand in his. "All that matters is you're okay."

I didn't understand what he was saying. 411? Was my brain still in pause?

"No one is going to hurt you," he continued.

"What are you saying?"

"She's gone now. Just rest."

"But I don't understand. What happened to me?"

"I'm not really sure." He looked down at the floor, avoiding my questioning eyes.

Grandpa shifted positions. We both glanced in his direction. Another snore, this time at a normal volume, and he was back asleep.

"You're not doing a report on coffeehouses, are you?" I asked.

"Not to worry about that now."

"Please tell me what's going on. I feel like I'm going insane."

"You're not. I'm in massive trouble."

Renn ran the back of his fingers along my cheek. Oh, God, did that feel good. Calming, yet inviting. The yearning sensation traveled through my entire body. My legs opened slightly, and a gasp escaped from deep inside me. No one in my whole life had ever touched me like that. I burned for him.

"Don't worry about me. Or Natasha. I have to go now. Before…" He paused, and I knew from the way he closed his eyes for a brief second, that he had changed his mind about what he was going to say. "Before your family gets back here."

"How do you know her? Natasha?"

"Soon. I'll tell you everything."

He stood up, but I held onto his hand. "Why don't you just vanish?" I waited a beat for his answer. When he didn't say anything, I kept talking. "Like you've been doing. And please don't lie."

I didn't like the way he looked at me, as if I had

opened up some secret box.

"Not by choice, Jessica."

"What do you mean? What's not your choice?"

I heard my aunt's voice down the hallway.

"I have to go." Renn kissed me quickly on the cheek. As he backed out of the room, he kept his eyes on mine.

Grandma and Aunt Beth found me sitting up, touching my cheek where Renn's hand had been just a minute before.

Had they seen him in the hallway? Or had he become invisible again?

"Jessie!" Grandma rushed to my bedside. "You're sitting up."

"I am." I smiled, trying not to let her see my confusion.

"Oh, sweetie. We were so worried." Aunt Beth set a cup of coffee, a muffin, and a packaged salad on the table near my grandfather and came up to the other side of the bed. "Has your grandfather been sleeping this whole time?"

I nodded. "He was awake for a minute, but yeah, mostly he's been sleeping."

"Morrie!" Grandma yelled at my grandfather. "Wake up."

"Uh? What? What's all the fuss about?" Grandpa lifted his head.

I smiled at him. He nodded at me.

"Has the doctor been here?" Aunt Beth asked, feeling my forehead. So silly, but so like Aunt Beth.

"No," I said, throwing off the covers.

"Jessie, be careful. You'll rip that out of your arm." Aunt Beth pressed the call button.

Once I was free from the IV and the catheter, I swung my legs over the side of the bed and stood up.

My legs weren't stiff or jelly-like. My vision was normal. Nothing sounded too loud. The lights weren't too bright.

I poured some water in a cup, listening for those musical notes, but all I heard was water, plain, normal water.

I wiggled my arms and legs for my aunt and grandmother. "See. Everything's fine," I lied. "I need to use the bathroom."

I stared at my face in the mirror. I was still me. My hair matted against the back of my head and my face was pale, but other than that, I still looked the same. Whatever had happened, there weren't any lasting effects. At least nothing physical.

I splashed cold water on my face and then called Lilly. She picked up immediately.

"Jess. Is that you? You're okay?"

"She's awake?" I heard Kyle in the background.

"Yes," Lilly said. "Be quiet so I can hear her."

"Where are you guys?" I asked.

"We're in the waiting area. Kyle's cousin is seeing if someone can test the fabric."

My heart lurched at the mention of the material.

"Don't say anything in front of Kyle. I saw him, Lilly. He came to the hospital and kissed me, and I'm okay now. Is that not the craziest thing ever?"

"Uh huh." She didn't sound convinced.

"How soon can you get back?" I asked.

"Give me the phone," Kyle demanded. "Let me talk to her."

"No."

I heard them arguing. I didn't want to talk to Kyle. I pressed the off button. It rang again immediately. I let it go to voicemail and left the bathroom.

Doctor Lawrence walked in, all smiles and happiness. She appeared genuinely surprised to see me walking around. And confused because she couldn't figure out what happened to me. Not a good sign for a doctor.

If I told her about Natasha's appearance and Renn's kiss, well, I'm sure she would have not only put me back in the bed but tied me to it. Aunt Beth and Grandma wouldn't be too pleased either, but then I wasn't about to tell anyone.

And I'd just have to take my chances on Grandpa. Even if he did mention what happened, no one would believe him.

After checking my vitals, Doctor Lawrence suggested I stay the night so she could monitor things. Just to be on the safe side.

Natasha's threatening eyes flashed across my mind. "No, I'm not staying here another night. Not even another hour."

"You have to listen to the doctor," Aunt Beth said.

"I do not have to stay. I know they can't make me." I walked over to the small closet and pulled out my clothes.

I reached inside my tank top for the material before I realized it was with Kyle. The room took a quick spin, and I grabbed the collar of the hospital gown.

"You are not fine." Aunt Beth steered me back to the bed.

"I'm as fine as I can be without that fabric," I said, feeling unbalanced. "It tells me…"

The doctor gave me a puzzled look and began typing quickly on the computer.

"What I mean is, it's special to me. I'm getting dressed, and I'm leaving."

Aunt Beth shot a concerned look at the doctor.

"I'm ordering a psych evaluation." Doctor Lawrence looked up from her computer.

"You can't keep me here," I said.

"We can if you're a danger to yourself or anyone else."

"I don't want to hurt anyone," I raised my voice. "Please, doctor. I just want to get out of here."

"Let's see how you are in a few hours." The doctor continued typing.

"Honestly," I said in a softer voice. "I don't like hospitals. I'm fine to go home."

"Jessie, sweetie," my grandmother said. "I think you should stay." I knew that voice all too well. She was worried about me and would do everything to convince me to stay one more night. I didn't have the energy to fight her.

I picked up my phone and texted Lilly.

—*Bring me a veggie from Taco Time. With hot sauce. 2 of them.*—

I walked over to the window and looked out onto the parking lot. The red line of sunset spread across the sky. Renn was somewhere out there.

Wanting him flowed through my bones, like a thirst that needed quenching. I pressed my head against the glass. The coolness seeped into my skin.

"You really should rest." Grandma straightened out the covers. "C'mon, sweetie. Get back into bed."

I didn't want to, but I climbed into bed in order to

please my grandmother.

"You guys don't have to stay here," I said, adjusting the horribly large pillow.

My phone beeped as I smoothed out the sheets. I read Lilly's text message. —*On the way. Fabric is weird. Kyle says Renn is a con man.*—

"Was that Lilly?" Aunt Beth asked, trying to read my text.

I set the phone on my lap, out of my aunt's line of vision. "They're on their way back. You guys can go, if you want."

"In a little bit," Grandma said.

I picked up the remote and turned on the six o'clock news for my grandparents to watch, so that I could mull over Lilly's text.

For the next few minutes, I pretended to watch the news while my grandfather snored, normal volume snorts, my aunt read her travel magazine, and my grandmother watched me.

Lilly and Kyle came back with burritos, tacos, and nachos. After a million hugs, they let me eat. I never thought junk food could taste so delicious.

When they finally got their act together to leave, Grandpa shuffled over to the side of the bed. He bent down to kiss me, steadying himself on the headboard.

"He's a nice fella," he whispered. "That one in the trench coat."

"Grandpa," I said. "You saw…"

He pressed a finger to his lips.

I watched my grandparents leave the room, my grandmother helping steady my grandfather.

"Aunt Beth," I said. "You should go, too."

"Not until I hear about this fabric. Where did you

take it, and what did they find?" my aunt asked, breaking a nacho in half before eating it.

I made eye contact with Lilly and shook my head slightly. She spoke just as Kyle started to say something. "Kyle's cousin is a chemist. He's testing it, and he'll call us tomorrow."

"Sure, tomorrow." Kyle played along, but his eyes were wider than normal, and I knew he wanted to spit out something bad about Renn.

"You look so tired, Aunt Beth. Please go home. Besides, don't you have to pack?"

"About that."

"Don't tell me you changed your mind?"

"We'll talk about that later. You're sure you'll be okay?" Aunt Beth finally made a move to leave, slinging her purse over her shoulder. "And you're going to stay?" She looked at Lilly.

"Until they kick me out," Lilly assured her. "I promise."

Once Aunt Beth was out the door, after rushing back in to get her sunglasses, I asked Kyle for the fabric.

He acted as if he hadn't heard me.

"C'mon," I said. "Give it to me."

"Jess, I don't trust this Renn guy." Kyle crossed his arms in front of his chest.

"I don't care. That's not the point."

He stood there like some mighty protector.

"And don't worry. He didn't give me drugs."

"What?" Kyle's jaw dropped open.

"Don't pretend you didn't say that, because I heard every word."

"You did?"

"It was stranage. I couldn't talk or move, but I heard everything." I held out my hand. "So, please give it to me."

Lilly tried to reach into Kyle's pocket, but he shoved her away.

"Wow. That was a big shock," Lilly said. "Since we're in a hospital, maybe you should see a neurosurgeon."

Kyle ignored her. "Why does this mean so much to you, anyway?" He held up a plastic bag with the fabric inside.

"It just does." I started to get out of bed.

"Okay. Relax. Here." He placed the bag in the palm of my hand.

I removed the fabric and held it between my fingers.

"You could hear us?" Kyle asked. "Everything?"

"Every single word," I said. "I thought I was moving. It sure felt like it. But I guess I wasn't. It was the scariest thing."

"Freaking weird." Kyle collapsed in the chair where my grandfather had been sitting. "I'm sorry I wasn't working this morning."

"I'm sorry you don't trust Renn," I said. "But Kyle, he hasn't done anything to hurt me."

"Yet," Kyle mumbled.

"Tell me, what did you find out? What's this made of anyway?"

"Some kind of fibers never seen before," Lilly said.

"So, it's something new." I ran my finger over the silk-like surface.

"Maybe. But my cousin, you know Chad, the one who works at that tabloid I told you about. He says that a Renn Porter doesn't even exist." Kyle said. "Besides Google, he used their tabloid databases. There's some actor and some old guy in Maine and it's a name on a TV show, but nothing that matches this guy." He looped his fingers together and cracked his knuckles.

The fabric started to warm up. Heat rushed through my body, from my fingers to my toes. Renn was on his way here.

Lilly saw me rubbing the material.

"Is it hot?" she mouthed.

I nodded that it was. "I could really go for a double shot mocha latte. Do you mind, Kyle? There's a Starbucks on the corner."

"And be a traitor?"

"I won't tell," I said, placing my hands in the prayer position.

"I'm on it." Kyle jiggled his keys, blew me a kiss.

"Get me the same as Jess," Lilly said as Kyle left the room.

"He's getting closer," I said to Lilly once I knew Kyle was out of earshot. "Go wait outside, in the lobby by the door, and text me as soon as you see Kyle coming back."

"Be careful, Jess. There is something strange about him. I don't think he's a con man or anything, like Kyle does. But you said yourself he vanishes. That's like being an alien, something non-human. Kyle does have a reason to be worried."

"Not about Renn. I haven't had a chance to tell you, but that horrible lady that came to The Hut, she showed up just a second before Renn. He saved me from her. So, I know I'll be fine with him."

"Text me if it gets weird." We hugged and then

Lilly left the room.

I quickly changed into my jeans and tank top. There was nothing sexy about a hospital gown. I slipped the fabric in my pocket and tried to sit casually on the edge of the bed.

Chapter Fourteen

Renn entered in jeans and a black long-sleeved shirt, his trench coat draped over his arm. My eyes riveted to his muscular arms and broad shoulders. I wanted them wrapped around me. I crossed my legs to stop them from shaking. It didn't help.

"Hello." He smiled, setting his coat on the chair. The overhead light bounced off the material, sending a prism of colors upward in a triangular shape.

"Hi."

He sat down next to me, brushing his fingers across my knee. If my insides had gone haywire with tingles and jitters from his kiss, they were now dancing off the chart. In this state, my heart monitor would have brought a flurry of nurses to my bedside. No doubt about it—there was something strong between us.

Kiss me.

He didn't. Not right away. Instead, he placed his hands on either side of my face and looked into my eyes. His mouth parted as he leaned forward gently touching my lips. Slowly his tongue found its way to mine.

We started to lie down, but before our bodies hit the mattress, he pulled away and sat up, leaving me wanting so much more. As well as completely shocked by his action.

He glanced at the fancy watch on his wrist. It held

a lot more information than the time. I twisted my head to get a better view of the icons on the watch's face. Noticing that I was staring, Renn quickly turned his arm over. A cluster of freckles, resembling a barcode in the shape of a T gathered beneath the clear watchband.

"When are they discharging you?" he asked.

I straightened my shirt. "Tomorrow. But I'm not staying tonight."

"You should stay."

"I am not spending any more time here than necessary."

He picked up my hand and held it between both of his. "It's easier to cam you if you're here."

"Cam me?" I asked.

"I mean, observe you," he said.

"What the hell is going on?"

I tried to pull my hand away, but Renn held it tightly between his.

"You disappear all the time. Poof. Just vanish. This crazy woman puts me in some suspended state. You get rid of her. Then leave. You want to cam me."

Renn took his eyes off mine and stared at the ceiling, as if the answers hung upside down like a family of bats. I didn't like the way his mouth pressed into a straight line. It gave me an uneasy feeling.

"Say something."

"Listen, Jessica. This is going to sound very…well, not something you're expecting to hear."

His Adam's apple went up and down as he sat collecting his words. After a minute, when he still hadn't told me anything, I started talking again.

"I can handle whatever it is you want to tell me."

His jaw tightened. He moved his lips. He squeezed

my hands tighter and stared at me for a few seconds before beginning. "I'm a matchmaker. Technically, still an apprentice."

"Not a reporter? A matchmaker?"

"Exactly. Someone who brings couples together."

"I know what a matchmaker is." I pulled my hand away.

"Yes, but our service is not what you know. It's somewhat like you have now, but there's no dating involved. It's more permanent."

"Right. That's what they all say. Anyways, what does this have to do with me?" My heart pumped fiercely.

He took the deepest breath and held it in for what seemed like forever. "Everything."

"I don't get what you're saying."

"Jessica, my company sent me here to get you for…"

"And kissing me is part of your job?" I stood up and started to walk away.

Renn grabbed my arm and turned me toward him. "Of course not. It turns out that the data I received from Central Match is incorrect."

"Central Match? Like Match.com?"

Renn snickered. "Please. Nothing so inferior as that."

"What makes your service so much better?"

He stared into my eyes. I couldn't turn away. My pulse beat in every part of my body.

"I'm just going to lay it all out for you," he said.

"Please do."

"I'm from the future. I'm on a mission. And I've broken the laws. That was not my initial intention. But after seeing you, it was my only course of action."

I simply stared at him. Too stunned to say anything.

"I work for a company called Time Traveling Matchmakers, Inc. Natasha is my boss."

I waited for him to tell me he was joking. He didn't.

"There's been a miscalculation. My behavior has placed me in massive trouble and…"

I held up my hand the way my aunt does when I talk too fast. "You said Time Traveling Matchmakers. As in time travel?"

"Exactly." He nodded.

Ohmygod. Here I am, thinking I met someone special. We have all this great chemistry. He's special, all right. Straight from a mental institution.

"So, we're good?"

I wanted to pinch his head between my hands and scream no. We were as far from good as we could get.

"Listen, if you're in trouble, I'll help you." I kept my voice calm. If he was mentally unstable, his reaction could be violent. "Somehow, you saved my life. You don't have to make up a story like this."

"I'm not deceiving you, Jessica."

"You think you're really from the future?"

"I know I am. Our organization was based on a famous movie. Actually, from your time."

"And who starred in this movie?" Two could play this game.

"I know it sounds like I'm concocting all this up…"

"What do you expect me to think? That you actually can time travel?" He really should be the one in the hospital bed.

"You wanted to know how I disappeared before. Well, that's how."

"You really are serious?"

"That was not meant to happen. I can usually control my traveling, but when we passed each other by the travel agency I was booted into a time stream. The same thing occurred this morning. I had to struggle to find my way back here. To you."

I bit my cheek. "This is crazy talk."

"Yes, I suppose it does sound like that." He stared into my eyes. "It's all true, whether you believe me or not."

I had seen him disappear. And unless he had taken some kind of invisibility-inducing drug or I had been in some hypnotic state, which I wasn't, what else was there to do but believe him?

But seriously, how could I believe him?

The insane thing was—I wanted to believe him. Every word. Which probably made me the crazy one.

"So, what exactly is your job?" I asked. Maybe learning more about it would make it easier to believe. "Tell me how it works."

"It's quite simple. We bring soul mates together," he said. "Usually to the future, but once in a while past-wards. You are, rather were, the subject of my mission."

My stomach twisted up like a wet dishrag. He has got to be kidding.

"You came here for me?"

Renn pressed his hand against mine, thumb against thumb, fingers to fingers. "Yes, but as I said, there's been a miscalc. You were matched incorrectly. I'm not taking you anywhere."

I started to answer him when he pulled me into his arms and kissed me. My senses bloomed. The throbbing between my legs become intense. I wanted him to touch me everywhere at once.

He moved his hand to my breast, caressing it gently at first. When I moaned, he touched me harder.

Oh, God. I wanted to crawl into the bed with him. I didn't care who saw us. It was insane to want someone like this, someone I barely knew, someone with time travel delusions.

"There," he said, pulling away. "Now do you believe me?"

"Yes, about this." I circled my finger along his chest. "Us, but not your crazy time travel talk. Who was I meant for, anyway?"

"That is of no consequence now. I knew from the very first day that something was wrong with my mission and…" He turned toward the door. "I hear your friends."

I didn't hear anything. Within seconds, my phone dinged, signaling a text message from Lilly.

—*Kyle's on his way up.*—

Renn and I jumped off the bed at the same time.

He placed his hands on either side of my face, rubbing his thumbs along my temples. "Promise me you'll stay indoors."

"What? Why?"

"For me."

Kyle's voice outside the room brought me back to reality. No telling what Kyle would do if he found Renn in my room. Or if he passed him in the hallway.

"Until tomorrow," he said, slipping on his coat and

heading for the exit.

"There's no time. Get in the bathroom." I pushed him inside and slammed the door.

I climbed back onto the bed, picked up the remote, and started channel surfing, not paying any attention to the images on the TV.

"Hey, there." Lilly hurried in first and sat down on the bed, flipping through a magazine, as if she'd been with me all along.

Kyle walked in a minute later. "You're all dressed." He handed both of us a latte. "Are you leaving?"

When he wasn't looking, I caught Lilly's eye and nodded toward the bathroom.

"Not yet. I just wanted to get out of that horrible gown." I took a long sip of the latte. It was decent but not as good as the ones we make.

"Listen, Jess." Kyle sat down on the other side of the bed. "I'm not being paranoid about all this. There's something about Renn I don't trust."

If you only knew.

"I hear you. And I understand your concern. But…"

"Hey, what's this doing down here?"

Kyle grabbed the fabric off the floor. Sparkles of light shot into the air. He let it drop to the ground.

"Did you see that?" Lilly asked, picking it up. "Oh. My. God. It's on fire."

It must have fallen out of my pocket when I got dressed. I reached out my hand. "Let me have it."

I rubbed my thumb over the smooth surface.

A clinking sound came from the bathroom. After that I didn't hear anything but the ripping through my body. The bed tilted. I grabbed onto the sides to steady myself.

When I looked up, Kyle was grabbing the fabric off the floor, just as he had done a few seconds ago.

"Hey, what's this doing down here?" he said. Sparkles flew into the air. He dropped the fabric.

"Did you see that?" Lilly said. "Oh. My. God. It's on fire."

I stared at both of them. They acted as if nothing was unusual.

"You guys, you just said all that."

"Said what?" Kyle asked.

"Time is repeating," I whispered. "It's happening like before."

My hands gripped the edges of the bed, crumpling the sheets. "I have to use the bathroom." I hurried to the door, opened it, and went inside.

The bathroom was empty.

****

The molecules settled around Renn as the world came into focus. He remained still, stabilizing his core. Breathe in, breathe out. Tighten the muscles, relax the mind. In. Out. Tighten. Relax. Become one with the surroundings.

He listened for the familiar music, indicating he had arrived at that wedding again. But he heard nothing except his own breathing.

Palm trees swayed above his head. His feet crunched into the sand. He listened for waves, but there didn't seem to be an ocean anywhere near him.

Stars crowded the night sky. Almost as if he could reach up and climb into them. He hadn't paid much attention in his astronomy classes, so the constellations were of no help in telling him where he had landed.

The air vibrated with a rhythm that at first sounded like singing, but then more like a seagull's cry.

His thoughts were a pile of puzzle pieces, his last solid memory having taken place inside the hospital bathroom. He had planned on hiding there until Jessica's friends left.

He had done nothing. And then without his control he'd spun into a time thread. And here he was. Wherever/whenever that might be.

This issue never came up in any of his classes. Time travel was controlled by the traveler. Only you and you alone. How many times had he heard his professors point to the class and recite those words?

He'd also studied case after case in *The Big Book* and had never read anything about unwanted traveling.

So, what the hell was happening to him?

It slipped into his mind that Arlianna hadn't sent a communication. He pulled up his sleeve. Holy crap. His locator wasn't on his wrist.

Never, under any circumstances, remove your locator. Rule #2.

Chapter Fifteen

Natasha watched Renn's blip on her screen. One nanosec it was beating like a heart and the next it froze into a straight line. She fired off five messages in a row, not receiving an answer for any of them.

That little snot faced baby. Why wasn't he answering?

First, he intercepts her retrieval of the subject, and now this. He's lucky the poor girl didn't die. Or perhaps maybe that would have been better. Then she could have had him arrested for violating the laws of Time Travel. And avoided this mess all together.

Natasha pressed the holocom on her desk. Her assistant's face rose up before her.

"Yes, ma'am," Lexi said.

"Check the connection on Renn Porter's locator."

Natasha watched Lexi as she followed her orders. At least someone always did what she asked.

"It's in a static position," Lexi said. "That means it's in one place."

"I know what that means," Natasha barked.

Lexi's face tightened, the line across her forehead deepening. "Of course, you do," Lexi's voice quivered. "I'll search for him."

"Let me know what you find." Natasha softened her voice. Despite her meekness, Lexi was the best assistant. Losing her would not be good.

Natasha turned back to her screen. Still no movement.

Law # 2- Never remove your locator.

Even the most naïve apprentice knew that. The locator functioned by reading the matchmaker's pulse.

How in the dickens would she ever find him? And then it dawned on her. How would he even find himself? His goose was cooked, as they used to say. How she loved those old-fashioned sayings. They expressed how one felt so much better than adjectives attached to cold, non-thinking computers. Or those stupid acronyms or images so popular in the modern world.

Well, she may not know where Renn had traveled, but she knew exactly where to find Jessica.

"Lexi, terminate Renn's locator. And prepare my meds," Natasha spoke into the holocom. "I'm leaving again to find Renn."

Chapter Sixteen

I sat down on the toilet because if I didn't, I knew my legs would buckle. It took me a second to realize the heavy breathing was my own. The thumping from my chest echoed in my ears. I was positive Kyle and Lilly could hear it on the other side of the door.

The ground sparkled. I reached down and picked up a small, circular disc. Strange icons moved on its surface. I tucked the disc inside my fist, inhaled Renn's lemony scent, and left the bathroom on rubbery legs.

Kyle rushed to my side. That familiar zing shot through my body as he grabbed my elbow and helped me onto the bed. As weird as it was, it felt good to know some things hadn't changed.

"What did he do to you?" Kyle leaned closer to my face. He inspected me as if I were a biology specimen.

"Nothing," I said. With my hand under the covers, my thumb worked itself back and forth across the disc.

"You can't fool me," Kyle said. "You look like shit."

"Thank you very much." I scooted lower under the covers.

"You know what I mean." Kyle checked the time on his cell phone, shaking his head as he shoved the phone back into his pocket.

"You have to be somewhere?" I asked.

He shrugged. "Nothing important."

I wanted him to leave. I wanted him to want to leave without feeling hurt. It's been the two of us ever since David dumped me, and I know Kyle likes to feel needed. Yet, at the moment, I needed to be alone with Lilly.

"Why don't you go?" I said, sounding as sweet as possible.

Kyle paced to the window and back.

"I did promise my brother I'd help him move a desk…"

"Go, then," I cut him off before he could make an excuse to stay.

"You'll call if you need me?"

"You know I will." I wouldn't.

The minute he left the room, Lilly turned to me. "Okay, spill it."

Sitting cross-legged on the bed, facing each other, I told her everything. I talked calmly right up to the most important fact.

"A time traveling matchmaker?" Her eyes took on the shape of full moons. "That's fucking unbelievable."

She stretched onto her side, resting her head on her elbow. She closed her eyes and pinched her lips together. A face she's been making ever since we were kids.

"He vanished from the bathroom," I said. "What else could it be?"

"Let me see that disc."

She ran her thumb over the surface. Just as it had done for me, a dozen or so icons took turns lighting up. "It looks like it's from a sci-fi movie. Like a prop."

I took it back from her. "I bet it's some kind of communication device." I tapped it with my fingernail.

It chirped, startling both of us.

My heart sped up, hoping it was a communication from Renn. But when the chirping stopped, one word flashed across the tiny screen. Deactivated.

There was nothing but icons. No keypad, no letters or numbers. I tapped on something that resembled a calendar. Immediately, the screen shimmered, and a 3-D *calendar appeared.*

7.1. – Lunch w/ Arl @ 2

7.08 Dinner w/ BFF

Buy 21st Century Slang Guide

7.10 Decide where to stay. Malibu Motel?

Get Stats fm Natasha

Stats?

"She's nasty looking." Lilly eyed the 3-D image of Natasha's face next to the memo. Hair pulled back tight, large round eyes, long nose, pencil thin lips. Her moving tattoo.

"You should see her in person."

"No thanks."

We read the last note together. *7.24 Leave for Mud Hut.*

I closed my fist around the disc. Its round edge burrowed into the cushioned part beneath my thumb.

7.24. The morning I had met Renn. All those moments rushed into my mind. The way Renn had handed me the glass of water, leveling the ground beneath me. How obsessed I had been watching him. The after-image that still haunted me.

Lilly put her hand on my arm. "What else is there?"

I pushed on an icon showing people talking to each other. Messages popped onto the screen.

To the right of each message was a 3-D icon of either Renn or Arlianna.

Renn – There's been a miscalc. Jessica is not Frank's Soulmate.

Arlianna – Central Match rarely makes a mistake.

Renn – Searching for flaws.

Arlianna – U R 2 raw.

Renn –My gut isn't

Arlianna – Do Ur job. She must be brought to Frank Griffin

I tossed the disc onto the bed. "Frank Griffin? Who the hell is he?"

"Sounds like he was supposed to be your soulmate."

I hit her on the head with the pillow.

Lilly picked up the disc. She sucked on her bottom lip, shaking her head. "Read this."

There was an exchange between Renn and an exquisite looking red-haired girl. Even the freckles walking across her nose added to her beauty. My heart thumped against my rib cage.

Tweetlyn – U haven't even left yet, and I miss U already

Renn – It's only 2 wks

Tweetlyn – Then U'll B gone again

Renn – U'll B busy with Ur career

Tweetlyn – AI doesn't compare to TT

Renn – But Ur 1 of the best

Tweetlyn – B careful. I L U

Renn – Me 2 C U in 2 wks.

I read the exchange over again. And then again. "He has a girlfriend."

"What does that even matter, Jess. He thinks he's

from the future."

Hot lava rose into my chest. "This is fucking crazy." I shrieked, feeling the veins in my neck pop out.

A nurse with a big happy face pin on her uniform appeared in the doorway. "Is everything okay in here?"

"All good," Lilly answered for me.

"I sat on the edge of the bed with my hands clasped tightly together. "The doctor said I could leave after a few hours. Are you getting my discharge papers?"

Happy Face checked my vitals and typed the information into the computer. "Everything looks good. I'll let the doctor know."

After the nurse left, I turned to Lilly. "What kind of game is he playing? Telling me he's a matchmaker and then kissing me but saying he shouldn't. Seriously."

"Not to mention, he thinks he's a time traveler."

I let out nervous giggle. "Yeah, that, too."

I stared at Lilly's face. Her mouth moved but the words were out of sync with her lips. I got off the bed, clutching the handrails.

"What is it?" Lilly asked.

Looking at her made me feel dizzy. I kept my eyes down. "It's like before. Your lips and words aren't together."

Lilly put her arm around me. "I've got you." Her voice sounded wavy. I couldn't tell if I was hearing it that way or her own fear was making it shake.

Commotion exploded at the nurse's stand. I peeked out the door. I got a glimpse of Natasha's stern face and the back of Arlianna's curly hair.

"It's them," I said. "We have to get out of here."

Chapter Seventeen

Spiders crawled under my skin as we rushed to the elevator. Halfway there, I stumbled. Lilly stopped me from falling. My legs tingled. With difficulty, I made it the rest of the way. I pressed the down button, over and over with my thumb. I bounced on the balls of my feet.

"C'mon. C'mon." The numbers lit up—slowly— one at a time.

Finally, it dinged, and the elevator arrived. I stumbled inside, and pushed the L. As the door closed, an orderly thrust her hand in the small space, forcing it to reopen.

She panted heavily, in time with my heartbeat. She smiled at me and moved closer to the wall. "They always keep it so cold in here."

Her mouth moved a second before I heard the words.

I clutched Lilly's arm.

When the elevator finally stopped, we hurried through the lobby and out the double doors toward the parking lot. The ground moved beneath me, thrusting me forward. My knees locked in place as I ran. Several times, I tripped over my own feet.

Opening the car door was almost impossible. My fingers slipped, breaking off the nail on my ring finger. My purse fell to the ground.

"You see them anywhere?" Lilly asked, as I finally

got into the passenger seat.

Her question made me laugh. "They're time travelers. They could pop up anywhere."

"Then why are we running?"

"Good question," I said. "It feels better to be moving."

Lilly drove as fast as she could, swerving several times to miss the parked cars. Five minutes later we sped toward our neighborhood.

"The nurses will be looking for you," Lilly said as we pulled into her driveway. This time her words and lips were back in sync.

"So what?" I chewed on the inside of my cheek. "I left without my papers. No big deal."

I decided it would be better to stay at Lilly's rather than my own apartment. Staying alone frightened me.

I flopped onto Lilly's bed, totally exhausted. I set the disc on her nightstand, but I kept the fabric in my pocket.

My brain caught up with my body. Once I put my head on her pillow, I could barely keep my eyes open. The past few days flashed through my mind. Renn. Natasha. The future. Time traveling. Maybe when I woke up, I'd discover this had all been a bad dream.

But maybe not.

****

From off in the distance Whitney Houston's voice reached his ears. "I wanna dance with somebody…" Despite his confusion, Renn found himself singing along, flashing back to his 20th Century Love Songs course, one of the mandatory classes for a Time Traveling Matchmaker.

If he'd had control over his travels, he would have

gone to one of Whitney's live concerts and not this beach affair. But something had spun him out of control, yet again.

Here he was at that same beach, the same wedding. And he had no idea why.

Out of habit, he kept touching his wrist. His locator had not magically reappeared. Not that he thought it would, but the action was comforting. Maybe somehow Arlianna would pick up his vibes, realize he was lost in time. It was better than obsessing over the alternative, being stuck in the past for the rest of his life.

That thought shot his heart into hyperdrive. His breathing became erratic. He realized he had stopped walking forward but was circling around inside his footsteps. None of this was helping him get back to Jessica.

He concentrated on calming his heart and regulating his breathing. If nothing else, he could control his bodily functions.

Keep walking. He watched his feet as they made impressions in the sand. Keep walking.

As he came to the clearing, the music softened into an instrumental, something he didn't recognize. He stood at the edge of the same clearing as before, staring at that large, white tent.

His body swayed, the world spun, quickly settling back in place. He needed food. And he needed it as soon as possible.

Trying to fit in, Renn walked with his head up, shoulders back toward the tent. Act like you belong, Arlianna had coached before he'd traveled on his mission. He'd had hours of practice. Weeks of reading had prepared him for the customs of Jessica's world.

Everything from the clothing to the obsession with social media.

This year where he had landed was about 1987 or so. Assuming he had his history correct. A time period he knew very little about.

A young woman came up beside him. "Friend of the bride or groom?" She wore a knee-length skirt with orange, black, and yellow stripes and a bright orange scoop-necked top.

"Groom," he answered, trying to sound natural as his mind skimmed through the pages of his Fashion Icons book.

"He's a strange guy," the girl said. "But they are so in love." She spread her hand across her heart and looked longingly toward the newlyweds holding hands as they walked onto the dance floor.

The bride looked familiar, but he didn't know exactly why. Something about the way she touched the strands of hair falling from the side of her bun. Or maybe the way she walked, a bit awkwardly, seemingly uncomfortable in all that white lace.

The groom looked out of place in his tux. Stiff as a mannequin. He was letting his bride lead him through the dance. Renn got the impression he would follow her anywhere.

When their dance was over, other couples joined them. Fearing the girl at his side would want him to dance with her, he excused himself and walked toward the buffet tables.

There was an overwhelming amount of pasta in a long silver dish. Several different types of salads. And dozens of long loaves of garlic bread. The smells bombarded his senses. He had to stop several times to steady his breathing.

Eating was crucial, but he couldn't take a chance on the salads. Roughage didn't agree with time travel. He decided to try the pasta. Reaching for a plate, he felt someone staring at him. The last thing he needed was to get busted for crashing a wedding. He turned away from the buffet table.

The band started playing again. The jitterbug melody brought everyone to their feet. Renn watched the bride and groom. The bride's bare feet were in perfect time to the beat. Once again, the sensation that he knew her from someplace swept over him.

The groom fit into his bride's curves like a puzzle piece. When the newlyweds broke away to talk to the other dancers, the new husband seemed confused and lost.

Out of habit, Renn looked at his wrist again. Empty, as before.

He would have to resort to old fashioned pen and paper, which he kept inside his trench coat pocket. He thought he'd never have to use it, but then he never thought he'd be spun out of control.

Law #20 – Keep pen and paper on hand for emergency data processing. Writing in any form helps brain functionality.

He wrote slowly, knowing he couldn't send this report. It would be useful for Central, when and if he was ever found. He was reminded of dozens of old movies where the stranded victim would record his daily activities. At least, it was something to do.

From the Log of Renn Porter
Mission# 265 – Griffin & Singleton
Day 3 PM

Arrivd at wedding again. Reason – unknown.

He chewed on the end of the pen. Looking up, he caught a glimpse of blonde, curly hair. Hair belonging to the one person he needed most in the world.

Arlianna moved toward him through a time travel mist.

Her chest heaved with the weight of a million angry words. All of which Renn was ready to accept.

Chapter Eighteen

I woke up in a completely dark room with my face inches from a wall. The smell of peaches lingered around me. Someone snored lightly at my side.

Panicking, I sat up and looked around.

Early morning sunlight crept between the blinds. Lilly's room took shape before my eyes. Soft peach candles lined her nightstand. The door to her walk-in closet stood ajar. Familiar portraits hung crookedly on her walls.

My heartbeat returned to normal. Near my side, I found the fabric. The material felt bone cold. I picked the disc off the nightstand. The face was black, probably in sleep mode, or something like that. The warmth from my thumb brought it to life. Icons appeared, but not as bright as yesterday.

Lilly's arm came out from under the covers and reached for her glasses. "What time is it?"

"Early." I glanced at her glowing digital clock. "Only ten after seven."

She sat up, hugging the quilt to her chin. "Did yesterday really happen?"

I held the disc in front of her face.

The icons began moving in a circular motion. I saw one that wasn't there before. It was a T shape, resembling the bar code on Renn's wrist. I pressed on it exposing a list of laws under the heading *Time*

Traveling Matchmaker's Handbook.

Some of the letters were fainter than others, but I could see enough to read it out loud. Understanding their meaning was another thing entirely.

Law #1 - The Trench Coat is the portal device that allows for Time Travel and then grounds the Traveler to his new surroundings. It may only be taken off for short periods of time.

Law #2 - Never, ever remove your Locator.

Law #3 - The TTMM must establish their CORE (Concentration, Orientation, Relaxation, Exhalation) through deep breathing exercises, before speaking.

Law #4 - It is imperative for the TTMM to consume water upon arrival in new time to avoid disorientation.

Law # 5 – To bring back the wrong person can cause much havoc in the lives of all connected parties.

Law #10 – The TTMM must read the entire file on the subject before their departure.

Law # 11 – The TTMM will never make a game out of traveling. There shall be no disappearing for shock value.

Law # 12 – If the TTMM takes oneself into an unknown time, they must immediately contact CM to receive a new directive

Law # 24 – The soulmate cannot be taken from within four walls. Transportation of a soulmate must be implemented in a large open area, with the sky as the ceiling

"What the fuck?"

I lifted my arm to throw the disc across the room.

Lilly grabbed my wrist. "Don't. You don't want it to break. Let's have some coffee." She took the disc from my clutched fingers.

"I need more than coffee," I said, getting out of bed and putting on my clothes.

"I don't think there's a drink strong enough for this," Lilly said. "We have flavored coffee, though. You still drink vanilla?"

"No lattes?" I teased.

I followed Lilly down the stairs and into the kitchen. Taking a seat at the counter, memories of our youth rushed at me. My mind was too full to appreciate them.

Lilly searched through a drawer of K-cups. "No vanilla. And no regular, either. Just decaf." She made a pouty face.

"No worries," I said. "I better go see my grandparents before they call the hospital."

"Call me if you need anything." Lilly spread out her pinky and thumb and held her hand to her ears.

I promised I would and then left her house. Although I wasn't about to tell my grandmother about Renn, I needed to see her reassuring face.

The branches of my tree swayed gently in the morning breeze.

"Do you really think Renn's a time traveler?" I asked. "Is he just some mentally deranged guy?"

The tree's limbs brushed the top of my head. I glanced at the tufts of green leaves, wondering if it existed in whatever year Renn thought he came from.

Once inside, I changed into sweats and a T-shirt and went into the main house to see my grandmother.

She looked up from the paper spread on the kitchen

table. "Jessie, sweetie. I didn't expect to see you. They discharged you already?"

I nodded and poured myself a cup of coffee.

"You feeling better?"

"Now that I'm out of that place," I said. "You know how much I hate hospitals."

Her white head bobbed up and down. I'm sure she was remembering those days after mom's accident just as I was. I wanted to put my arms around her, but my lying got in the way.

After everything she's done for me, she deserved the truth. I promised myself that once this was all over, I would tell her everything. For now, seeing her face was enough to get me through the day.

"I'm going to shower," I said. "Coffee's good this morning."

"I'm going to the market later," she said. I could hear the worry in her voice. "Let me know if you need anything."

I left her reading the paper and went back to my apartment.

An unbearable urge to know my mother confronted me as I stared at her photo on my dresser.

"Mom," I said to her face. "What do you think about Renn? Do you believe him?"

I thought of a time when my mom read to me. I had missed school. She had read a fairy tale changing her voice with each character.

If I really think about it, that's my one solid memory.

Throughout the years, my father has filled in the gaps with so many stories of my mom they feel like my own memories.

But that day was mine. She made the characters come alive, and I believed in the impossible. Time traveling didn't stray far from those make-believe ideas. If it were really possible, could I travel back to see her again?

I took the disc from my pocket. The icons were visible, but barely.

My cell phone buzzed. I was tempted to let it go unanswered.

"Hey, Kyle," I said.

"I called the hospital, and they said you were discharged."

"Yeah?" I waited for Kyle to ask for more details.

"That's good," he said. "What did the doctors have to say?"

"Dehydration. Exhaustion. Nothing serious."

I knew Kyle knew I was lying, but I let it go.

"Are you up for the beach today?" I reached into my pocket, rubbing the fabric. Not that Renn would be sitting in his motel room, but it was worth a try. After yesterday, I would love getting out of the Valley. "Get some lunch. How does that sound?"

"Whatever you want, Jess."

"Renn didn't do this to me," I said. "I really need you to believe me."

"Maybe he is one of the good ones," Kyle said. "I just don't want to see you go through another horrible breakup."

"I know."

We planned on leaving around eleven. If Law # 24 was right, I would be safe unless I was out in the open.

Oh my God. I was actually giving credibility to those laws.

Every time I thought how absolutely crazy it was to believe Renn was really from the future, the empty bathroom reminded me he had disappeared into another dimension.

****

I loved driving through Topanga Canyon with all its curves and turns. In certain places, the density of the trees blocked the sun completely. Then we'd go around a corner, and a buttery sunlight would bath us in its warm glow.

Years ago, Lilly and I imagined living in one of the small houses tucked away from the street. She'd work on her photography while I wrote screenplays.

But that was then.

"Looks like you have at least a week off," Kyle said, taking a curve faster than I liked.

I grabbed onto the overhead handle.

Up ahead, the Pacific Ocean spread before us like a rolling blanket covered with twinkling diamonds. The view filled me with hope and promises of good things, causing my mood to lift. Maybe Renn would be in his motel room.

I wondered why his company put him up so far from The Mud Hut. Or maybe it didn't matter, because he time traveled.

"What do you feel like eating?" Kyle's question registered in the back of my mind. Way, way back there.

"Jess? Did you hear me?"

"Just thinking." I pulled the fabric from my pocket.

"Shrimp tacos? Pasta?'

"What?" I turned away from the window and faced Kyle.

"You're not even listening to me."

"I'm sorry," I said. "I can't get Renn off my mind. I know you don't like him, but—"

"I don't trust him," Kyle interrupted. "He could be a good guy. I just don't know yet."

I looked away from Kyle and out my window at the hillside. We passed a spot of bare dirt. Although I loved the Santa Ana winds, they always seemed to kick fires into high gear and destroy the beautiful landscape along the Pacific Coast Highway.

Out of the corner of my eye, I could see Kyle stealing glances at me.

"Watch out!" I shouted. "Everyone is stopping."

Kyle slammed on the brakes. I jerked forward, the seat belt pinching my armpit. "Geesh, Kyle. Watch the road. Besides, aren't you happy I'm not obsessing over David anymore?"

"Honestly, I'm not so sure."

We passed the Malibu pier and then, up on our right, there was a shopping center. I hadn't seen a motel anywhere. Just several fancy hotels with fantastic beach front views. Maybe he had decided to stay somewhere else.

"We passed most of the restaurants," Kyle said.

"Keep going. We can always turn around."

A mile later, I saw the motel.

"Here. Here," I forced my words at Kyle. "Pull into that Beach Mini Mart. Next to that motel. Let's just get some water and snacks and take a walk on the beach."

Kyle made a sharp turn into the parking lot.

"Go on in," I said. "I'll be right there. I have to send Lilly a text."

"What is up with you today?" Kyle said.

127

"Go. I'll meet you inside."

Once Kyle entered the mini mart, I headed for the motel.

Red plastic chairs sat in the lobby on either side of a glass table. The place smelled like ammonia mixed with pine. Of all the beautiful hotels along the coast, why would anyone want to stay here?

A boy with horrible acne stood behind the front desk. His lips began to move, but the words didn't come out for a few seconds. "Can I help you?"

I placed my hands on the counter to steady myself.

The boy leaned forward. "Miss, do you want a room?"

I forced myself to keep my eyes off his face. It made me less dizzy not to look at him.

"Do you have a Renn Porter here?" I asked, looking at a crack on the counter.

"I'm sorry. I can't give you that information."

I pulled a twenty-dollar bill from my wallet. "Now can you?"

The boy grabbed the money and typed quickly on his computer.

I bounced on the balls of my feet, chewing on the inside of my mouth. Turning away from him, I looked up. A blurry reflection showed in the glass behind his head. As I stared, Natasha's harsh face came into focus. Her heart tattoo shifted into those two heads. I gasped, throwing my hand over my mouth, and turned around.

She wasn't behind me. I turned back to the clerk. The image vanished. With my head ringing, I dashed from the motel toward the liquor store. I tripped two times before pushing on the glass door with the palm of my hand. Kyle stood in line at the register.

I grabbed his arm. "Let's go."

"I thought you wanted this stuff."

Everything was way out of sync. The package of chips rustled a second after Kyle squeezed the package.

"Just leave it." I grabbed the bottles of water and bags of chips out of his hands and set them on the counter. "C'mon."

"Jess. You're the one who…"

I pulled him out of the store and toward his truck. My own feet kept getting in my way. My legs weren't moving properly, but there was no time to waste.

Natasha stood in front of the motel—arms crossed in front of her chest. Her trench coat flapped open in the sea breeze. Her eyes spoke death, aiming straight for my heart.

"Hurry, unlock the door," I said, looking down.

"What's wrong?"

I saw the door unlock, and then I heard the click.

"That lady? See her over there in the trench coat?"

I looked at the door handle as I opened it.

"What lady?" Kyle asked.

"She's standing right in front of that motel sign."

"There's no one there."

I looked up. Kyle was right. There was no one standing there. Not now. But I could see her haunting image in my mind.

"Check your backseat? Make sure it's empty."

"What? Are you out of your mind?"

"Just do it, please."

After rolling his eyes, he peeked into the back of his truck. "All clear."

"Thanks." I got in quickly, slammed and locked the door. As if that would keep her out. At least, she couldn't take me away, but that didn't mean she couldn't put me back in that suspended state.

"You're acting crazy."

"Maybe," I mumbled.

"There is no maybe." He started the engine.

"Go." I bounced in the seat.

"Not until you tell me what's going on in that head of yours."

"Drive, please." I pulled my legs up on the seat and wrapped my arms around them.

"That thing started happening again. Everything was out of sync."

"So, you are having effects from that coma. You're seeing things again."

"I'm not seeing things. That's not what I said."

"What about the lady you thought you saw?"

"I did see her."

The ride home lasted forever. I crossed my legs and uncrossed them. Finally, I tucked them under my butt. I picked at my fingernails and closed my eyes, feeling the sun blink against my lids.

"You need an MRI," Kyle said, pulling into my driveway.

"My brain scan was fine."

"But not everything is known about comas. You could be having visions, and who knows what else could happen."

"Listen. I wasn't in a coma." I faced him. "You've got to get that through your brain."

Kyle rested his arm on the back of the seat, his fingers tapping lightly on the vinyl. "I couldn't stand it if anything happened to you."

I smiled at him. "I wouldn't want anything to

happen to you, either." I touched his arm quickly, feeling a slight zing. "Thanks for bringing me home. Sorry for acting so weird."

"You want company?"

"Not now. I'll call you"

Before getting out of the car, I looked at Lilly's front yard and at the Barnvelds' who lived on the other side of us.

Lilly's lawn was a smooth green, a true indication of how things worked in her household. The Barnvelds had replaced their lawn for rocks and cactus. My grandmother always called them a practical bunch. Our front yard was a patchwork of different shades of brown and yellow, with some green fighting for life, much like my heart.

Don't forget to call," Kyle said as I opened the door.

"Of course." I bit the inside of my lip as I ran into the main house.

Chapter Nineteen

Renn sat on the edge of his lumpy motel bed, waiting for Arlianna to speak. She sat across from him in the lone chair.

After approaching him at that beach wedding she had handed him a new locator and demanded he meet her in Malibu. That was that. And here they were.

"This place leaves something to be desired," Arlianna said.

He wanted to tell her he hadn't chosen this motel, but he didn't want to be disrespectful. His behavior was causing enough trouble.

He crossed the room to the tiny fridge, got a bottle of water, and placed it on the table in front of her. Staying hydrated was a crucial aspect to time travel. **Law #4.** He wished he'd had some oranges, one of Arlianna's favorite foods, but he hadn't been expecting her to visit.

As for his immediate future, he expected her to yell at him, go off the handle as they used to say. But she said nothing.

She acknowledged the water with a nod, letting it sit untouched.

With every second that ticked by, the motel air became harder for him to breathe. It grew thick with Arlianna's disappointment. He was her apprentice, her star pupil. She had put her faith in him. And he had let her down.

"There are flaws," Arlianna finally said, staring directly into his eyes.

Renn nodded, feeling the slightest glimmer of hope.

"You must return home."

The glimmer slammed shut. "I can't," he blurted out.

Arlianna held up her hand.

"I'm sorry. I didn't mean to disagree. But you have to understand. There's this…" He held an imaginary ball in front of his face. He swallowed his words. **Rule #13 – Never disobey one's mentor.**

"Go on," she said.

"You must know what it is. You said yourself there were flaws."

"I only know that the subject—"

"Please call her Jessica."

Arlianna's face softened. "I know that Jessica and Frank are not soulmates."

"That's because I'm her soulmate." Renn held a fist to his chest. "I know it in my heart and gut."

Arlianna closed her eyes, slowly exhaling. "I thought as much."

"You knew?"

"No, of course not. But I know now."

"Why did Natasha do this?" Renn asked. "Why would she send me after my own soulmate?"

"I'm not sure it was on purpose." Arlianna took a sip of the water.

"But she had to know Frank and Jessica are not a match."

"Yes. I've been suspecting her of foul play. But I

didn't think she'd do it with me involved."

"We can't let her get away with this," Renn said.

"I will handle Natasha. You must return home and accept another mission."

"I can't do that."

"You must. If you want to remain employed."

Renn mulled over her ultimatum. Remaining a matchmaker was out of the question. He couldn't work for such a conniving person.

"How can you still work for her?" he asked.

Arlianna ran a finger through her curly hair. "There is a lot of history between us."

"But she's trying to harm Jessica." Renn paced the small room.

"I know," Arlianna said. "But it's imperative we follow the proper channels."

"And if I don't go home?" he said.

"I can't protect you any longer."

He opened the door to his motel, letting in the sea breeze. He ached for Jessica. He'd never be able to think straight if he didn't see her again.

From the compassion showing on his mentor's face, her sad smile and half-closed eyes, Renn knew she was thinking the same thing.

Chapter Twenty

I stared at the sliver of moon hanging in the sky.

"Perfectly fitting, don't you think?" I said to my tree. "Just like me. I'm a sliver of myself." The tree stood perfectly still in the night air. Her branches silhouetted against the sky.

What if Renn was gone forever? What would I do with my life if he never came back? Ever.

Ever was a word that didn't do well alone. It goes much better with *happily* and *after*. The way my life used to be. The way I thought it never would be again after David, and then along came Renn. And the world opened up, even better than before.

His lips. His touch. His eyes. His voice. There wasn't room in my mind for thoughts of anything else.

My hunger for Renn overpowered everything. It didn't matter that he claimed he came from the future. Maybe he did. So many things in this world defy logic. Especially love.

Fifteen steps from my tree to my bathroom. Thirteen steps from the bathroom to the kitchen. *Please, God, bring him back to me.*

I opened and closed my fridge. A hunk of cheese, some old apples, and a quart of milk occupied the bottom shelf. Nothing too enticing.

My stomach growled. I opened the fridge again and picked up the healthiest looking apple, one without any bruises. Although, it didn't matter. I probably wouldn't each much, anyway. I might never eat another decent meal. I'd wither away, waiting for someone who might never show up.

The apple tasted sour. I spit the skin into my hand and tossed the whole thing in the trash. The fabric in my pocket grew warm.

"Jessica."

I spun around.

Renn smiled at me from across the doorway. He leaned against the wall, his trench coat open to expose a silky blue shirt. His lemony scent drifted into the room.

"It's you," I said, stating the obvious and feeling foolish for doing so.

His smile filled me with lightness.

"It's me," he said, as if he'd just returned from the store. In fact, he held a bag of donuts.

Donuts! He vanishes out of the bathroom and materializes out of thin air the next day with donuts?

A second later, the bag fell to the ground, and I was in his arms, kissing him. Putting the ever back into my life.

****

If Renn had any doubt, even the slightest bit, it had vanished with Jessica's smile. She lit up his entire being.

No question he looked ridiculous holding a bag of donuts, but social etiquette demanded he bring something as an apology. The bakery was the only place open.

Now, several hours later, after being lost in their lovemaking, he sat outside her door, staring at the most amazing tree. Her essence spoke to him. He couldn't say why, but he felt certain the tree was a female.

Every time he looked at her leafy branches, she swept down across his head, as if she was mothering him. A drop of sap wet his arm, tiny as a falling tear.

As Arlianna had said, his life was in his hands. He knew what he had to do.

Jessica would not be anywhere, with anyone, but him. He had convinced Arlianna to give him twenty-four hours to figure out his future. After that, she would be forced to report him AWOL from his mission.

This world may be different from the one he knew, but not when it came to love. The heart still beat to the rhythm of desire and yearning. No amount of technological advances could change that.

He tapped on his locator, opening the icon of his personal journal. On second thought, he closed the icon and pulled out his pen and paper.

From the Personal Journal of Renn Porter

Stars dot the sky like powdered sugar.

Jessica talked me into her bed rather easily. Made love like it's supposed to be made.

Burning. Hot. Desire. Can't get enough. My tongue on her skin. Salty. Spiced with lust. Thrusting inside her I thought I would lose my mind. Maybe I did.

Making love has never been like this for me.

I want to stay in this time, this place 4ever. But not yet. I must inform Jessica although it will pain me to do so.

Natasha must not get away with her false matches. Her destiny lies in my hands.

Chapter Twenty-One

Early morning sun filtered through the branches of my tree. I reached over to make sure last night had not been a dream. My hand touched the empty mattress.

I closed my eyes, letting the tears seep out. But before I could imagine the worst, a hint of lemon drifted my way, followed by footsteps.

"Jessica, are you awake?"

"You're still here?" I sat up, looking toward my open door. Renn walked in carrying a mug.

"Of course. It's a lovely morning." He poured a coffee for me, adding a dash of cream, and then motioned for me to join him outside.

I couldn't get up fast enough.

"The way you like it?" Renn handed me a mug of coffee. I sat down next to him on the porch swing. "Perfect." The fabric in my pocket threw off a pleasant heat.

"You look utterly irresistible." Renn ran his thumb over the top of my hand. The warm sensation ran up my arm, filling my entire body.

My neck and cheeks burned carrying me back to our night of lovemaking. Major fireworks had exploded inside me. The kind that movies are made of. He touched me in places that I didn't even know had feelings. Behind my knees, along my elbows, in the small crevice at the base of my spine. And my marks on his back, well they will be there for days.

Passion and desire breathed between us, weaving us as one. He couldn't possibly have a girlfriend back in his time. Still, I needed to know for sure.

"What?" Renn asked. "You look like you want to ask me something."

"I saw this girl on that disc thing you left behind," I asked. "Who is she?"

"Holy crap, Jessica. You have my locator?"

"If that's what you call it, yeah."

"Why didn't you tell me?" His voice held a ring of anger.

"I didn't know what it was. I found it in the bathroom after you disappeared."

He covered his forehead with his hand. "It must have snagged on something."

"So, don't accuse me."

"I'm not. It's just never fallen off before. Luckily, Arlianna has enough clout. She ordered me a new one and somehow found me. But, my God, why didn't you say something?"

I pushed my thumb against my cheek.

"Jessica, why didn't you tell me you…"

"I told you, I didn't know what it—"

"You had to know it was mine."

"But you didn't answer me. Who is she? That girl."

He rested his hand on my thigh.

"A friend," he said. He squeezed my hand. "She's a friend."

"How would I know that? I know nothing about you. For all I know that girl could have been your wife." I could feel the tears starting. "Why did you leave from the bathroom, anyway? I just wanted you to hide there until my friends left."

"It was not of my doing. Literally. I was booted into a time stream. I didn't plan on departing like that."

"Something just up and pulled you away?"

"Exactly," he answered. "Maybe my locator went orbital on me. I don't know."

"What's going on, Renn?" I stared into his eyes, afraid of the secrets behind them. "Please tell me."

"I think you know." He picked up my hand and placed it on his heart.

I leaned forward to kiss him, but kissing wasn't going to get me the answers I needed.

"I know we have this…" I squeezed his hand. "But all that other stuff."

"You're not this guy Frank's soulmate. We've already established that." He touched my cheek and then ran his finger over my lips.

"But—"

He stopped me with a kiss. So delicious, leaving me wanting way more.

"We're soulmates, Jessica. I don't need any Central Match or data synchronizer to tell me that."

I nodded my head as tears got mixed up in my smile. I reached up and touched his hair, so soft and silky. "Okay, but if it's your job to match people, why did Natasha send you to get me for someone else?"

Renn gave the swing a push. "That's the big question. So far, all we know, Arlianna and I, is that Natasha will do anything for credits, or money as you call it here in this time." He rubbed his thumb and forefinger together. "She's made false matches in the past, sending a Matchmaker after the wrong person."

"So that's what she's doing now? Just for the money?"

"I believe so. I heard rumors about some investments she's made where she's taken some hard losses. As soon as I questioned her authority, by saying I saw flaws, she demanded I bring you immediately."

"But why me?"

"That I don't know. Possibly just some random choice. I doubt she knew we were soulmates."

"But wouldn't that show up on her Match thing? You and me?"

"It's not a hundred percent correct. After all, it was programmed by humans. All I can say is I'm glad Natasha sent me and not someone else who would have taken you. And then we…" I watched his Adam's apple move up and down. "We wouldn't have ever met."

"So now what?" A breeze blew across the porch. The rustling of the leaves was a close second to the stirring of my heart.

Renn looked at his feet as they pushed against the pavement. "We have to keep you safe. Natasha will come for you."

"I saw her yesterday," I said.

He brought the swing to a halt. "I told you to stay inside."

"You left, without a word. What was I supposed to do? I thought you were never coming back."

He stood up and paced around the porch. "I told you. I didn't plan on departing. And I wasn't off having fun. I was lost and trying to get back here. If not for Arlianna, I'd still be wandering around in 1987."

I stood next to him, gently touching his arm.

"Where was Natasha?" he asked.

"At the beach. And I wasn't alone. I was with Kyle."

Renn's body stiffened. "He likes you."

"He's a good friend."

"He wishes you were his soulmate." Renn put his hands on either side of my face and stared into my eyes. "But it won't work. You and I are meant for each other."

"I don't want to be with Kyle. We really are just good...best friends," I said, placing my hand on top of his, ready to kiss him and make love right there on the porch. "We tried dating. It's not there for us."

"For you."

"For both of us. Kyle's a romantic. He just wants to be in love."

"And I want you," he said. "I want to stay."

But.

The word ballooned between us. The air grew thick with our silence as he looked away from my face and down at the ground.

"You're going to leave, aren't you?"

"I have to, Jessica."

And just like that my world crashed around me. Again. No. No. No. I wasn't going to let that happen. I turned and opened my apartment door.

He grabbed my arm, pulling me back toward him.

"This is not what I want either," he said. "But Natasha must be stopped."

Pressure built up behind my eyes.

Without answering, Renn walked toward my tree. Her branches seemed to bend to meet him as he picked off a few leaves.

He walked back toward me, kissed the leaves, and

tucked them into my hand. "While I'm gone, promise me, you won't go outdoors."

"That's insane," I said.

"Then don't go alone and only when necessary."

"Why should I promise you anything?"

"Because," Renn said. "I want you to be safe from Natasha."

"That doesn't make sense. She came into my hospital room, didn't she?"

"Yes, but she couldn't do anything but scare you."

"She did a good job of that."

Two birds flew between the tree branches, chirping to each other. It sounded like they were arguing. If birds even disagreed.

"How long? A day? Two weeks? A month? How do I know I'll ever see you again?"

"Time is irrelevant," he said.

"For you maybe." I reached into my pocket. At least I still had the fabric and would know when he was coming back. I ran my thumb over its silky surface.

"This is…" His eyes opened wide, and he stepped backward reaching out his hand. "Jessica. Something is happening to me. I'm…"

A pain ripped through my body. I stumbled backward, with my arm behind me. My hand stopped me from falling flat on my butt. Rubbing my wrist, I sat up. "Renn?"

I twisted to look behind me.

"Renn? Where are you?" I called.

I smelled the lemony air, but he was nowhere around.

Those same two birds flew by, chirping their angry chirps.

Unable to move, I stretched out on my back and stared up at the sky. It was a warm, cloudless morning.

Wherever Renn had gone, I took comfort in knowing we looked at the same sky. Or at least I hoped we did. I assumed whatever time he was in the universe hadn't become unrecognizable.

"Promise me you won't go outdoors alone." What a crock. He had left me alone, not the other way around.

I waited a few more minutes, hoping he would return. He didn't. I dragged myself into my apartment.

My journal sat on my nightstand. A reminder that my adviser was waiting for my film project. I started writing.

The way he kisses me is like nothing I've ever felt before. He says we're soulmates and that this is our destiny. But he keeps disappearing to a place I can't follow.

I wrote fast and furiously for most of the day. Taking a few breaks to check on my grandparents and eat a quick dinner. By evening, I had added another twenty pages. My idea was taking shape, while my heart was losing its edges.

Chapter Twenty-Two

My side burned, hotter than it ever felt before. I bolted upright, expecting to see Renn. He wasn't there and neither was his scent.

But I knew he was close.

The digital clock on my dresser flashed 2:15. I had fallen asleep, which I had thought impossible, my mind consumed with thoughts of him.

I grabbed a sweatshirt off the back of my chair, slipped it on, and waited for Renn to appear.

The clock flipped to 2:16. 2:17. 2:18.

Unable to sit still, I headed into the main house, knowing he would have no trouble finding me.

The kitchen was empty. As was the living room. I opened the sliding door that led to the backyard and stepped outside.

Other than the gurgling of the pool filter, the night was quiet. Almost too quiet. My grandparents slept with their window open. I should hear my grandfather snoring.

I walked toward their room, bumping into a patio chair. I heard it scrape against the ground, several seconds after it moved. Natasha was also nearby.

My breath stuck in my throat. Adrenalin mixed with fear burned through me.

Stay within four walls. Renn's voice echoed in my head.

The garage was closer than the house. My fingers fumbled with the doorknob.

Turn. Open.

Something pounded in my ears. It took me a second to realize it was my own heart.

I grabbed the knob with both hands, forced it to the left, and stepped into the dark space. A tan fabric shimmered in the corner, near my grandmother's old filing cabinet.

"Hi, Jessica."

This was not who I expected.

Arlianna walked slowly toward me. Her blonde curly hair framed her face like a halo. Her coat rustled in a melodic sort of way. And although she had a warm, inviting smile, she wasn't who I wanted to be with right now.

"Where's Renn?" I asked, touching the cooling fabric. "He was here. I could feel him."

Arlianna nodded. The tattoo on her ear transformed from a flower into a heart. I couldn't stop staring at it. "He was. I had him leave."

"Why?"

Arlianna put her arm around me. "Let me explain. I'm going to turn off my locator. You have to listen without interrupting me. I can only leave it off for a few minutes."

"I don't understand."

She silenced me by holding up her hand.

"We all work for the same organization," Arlianna began. "Renn is completely correct about Natasha, which puts him in grave danger. Natasha followed him here. I intercepted before she got to him and convinced her that I should be the one to terminate Renn's apprenticeship and bring you myself. But it won't take long for her to figure out that I betrayed her. And that Renn is on his way to the board to report her misconduct." She glanced at her wrist.

"Is he going there now?" I asked, taking the cold fabric from my pocket.

"What is *that*?" Arlianna stepped toward me. Her eyes narrowed, and a deep line appeared on her forehead.

"Nothing." I turned away.

Arlianna snatched the material from my fingers so quickly I had no time to think.

"Give it back to me." I said, reaching for the fabric. "It's not yours."

"Yes, it is," I insisted.

Arlianna rubbed the fabric between her fingers. Her motion made the room spin. I felt sick to my stomach.

"This explains why he's been losing his control. You can't keep this, Jessica. If you touch this while in Renn's presence, he time travels."

"But…"

"But nothing." She tucked it in the pocket of her trench coat. "He can't travel without having control of his destination."

"I won't touch it when he's around," I said. "I promise. I won't."

"That would be impossible."

"Please. I promise."

"Next time he gets booted into a time stream I may not be able to rescue him." Her eyes softened as she spoke.

147

Without the fabric, a giant hole sat inside me. I'd never know when Renn was nearby.

"Renn will be back," Arlianna said. "Go about your life. Stay indoors as much as possible. You can't be taken from within four walls." She tapped her wrist. "Go back to the house. I'll watch to see that you get there safely."

I just stood there.

"Go," she said. I knew she was trying to help. But I couldn't move without the fabric. "Go." She repeated.

I remained still.

"You're not helping him by resisting me."

I took two small steps. "He'll be okay?"

Arlianna smiled. "He's going to be fine."

I walked slowly toward the house, leaving part of me behind. I had no choice but to believe her. Back in my room, I picked up Renn's disc. The icons shifted back and forth, barely visible. I didn't have much time before they would disappear completely.

I opened the *Handbook*, searching for something in the laws that might indicate where Renn would be, or if he would be returning.

Law # 9 – The TTMM must learn the correct lingo before traveling

Law # 15 - The TTMM must submit a report each PM.

Law # 17 – Tampering with another TTMM's portal device is grounds for imprisonment.

Law # 25 - Those people with higher-than-normal energy levels cannot time travel. And will prohibit others from traveling by physical contact.

I read number #25 repeatedly, thinking of Kyle. A person with his condition will prohibit time travel.

Being with him would keep me safe. I knew I could count on him, despite his doubts about Renn. Maybe, even more so, because he was so sure Renn was dangerous.

In any case, we've always been there for each other. There was no reason for me to doubt he'd be there for me now.

****

Renn didn't waste time wondering where he was. He knew his exact location. Why didn't matter. All that mattered was getting back to Jessica.

He tapped his new locator, sending an urgent communication to his mentor.

Arlianna: Again?

Renn: Yes. Why am I traveling to this wedding?

Arlianna: I don't know. You must orbit. Leave. I'll keep Jessica safe.

Renn: I must see her.

Arlianna: We'll talk.

Once back at the dingy motel, Renn sat on the plastic chair in front of his door, facing the ocean. The traffic on Pacific Coast Highway made it difficult to hear the waves. But he knew they were rolling in and rolling out. Just as he knew Jessica was wondering and worrying about him.

He was thankful Arlianna had saved him again. He appreciated everything she'd done for him. From getting him into the Time Traveling Matchmaker's organization, to praising him at the annual dinners and accepting him as her apprentice.

But now he was forced to go against her wishes. He was not going to orbit until this whole messy situation blew over.

He was going to see Jessica once more before returning home. And once home, he was going to accuse Natasha of tampering with time travel matches, a sure ground for her imprisonment.

"I'm sorry, Arlianna," he whispered to himself.

His mentor had tried to convince him not to return to Jessica, to let her sort things out with Natasha. Arlianna promised to keep Jessica safe, but he needed more than safe. He needed to kiss Jessica, hold her in his arms, and make her believe with all her heart and soul that he would not be leaving forever.

Chapter Twenty-Three

"You didn't bring the girl with you?" Natasha stared across her desk, locking eyes with Arlianna, this woman she despised more than any other.

"Obviously, not," Arlianna said. "I couldn't lure her outside."

"That's bull crap. If anyone can lure a subject beneath the sky, it's you." Natasha pressed her holocom, turning off the system. The last thing she needed was for Lexi to overhear.

"It wasn't the proper time." Arlianna picked up one of Natasha's old-fashioned pencils, something she always did to irk Natasha.

But today, Natasha wasn't going to let it get to her.

"Well, if anyone knows about timing, it's you." Natasha knew they were both thinking about the time Arlianna caught her in bed with Seth.

Not that she wasn't happy with Seth now. But back then, it was more lust than love. A one-night stand that should never have been. She had planned on never seeing him again, with Mason being none the wiser.

But Arlianna, with her goody two shoes honesty had convinced Natasha to confess to her fiancé. No one should start a marriage with secrets. Arlianna was sure Mason would be forgiving. What bull. Once Mason knew Natasha had been unfaithful, that was the end.

"How many times do I have to tell you I'm sorry?

My God, Nat, it's been twenty years. I didn't think Mason would call off the wedding." She leaned forward, setting her elbows on Natasha's desk.

"No, you didn't think at all." Natasha twirled her chair around, keeping her back to Arlianna.

"That's not true. I thought he'd understand. I was saving you from starting off your marriage with a lie. Something you wouldn't have been able to live with, and you know I'm right. Or you did back then."

Natasha spun back around. "All I knew was I loved Mason more than life itself. You were my friend, and I trusted you. I looked up to you. I believed you."

Arlianna rose from her chair. "Oh, Nat, that's bull. If you had loved Mason, you wouldn't have slept with Seth. And if Mason really loved you, it would have worked out. He wouldn't have cared about a one-night fling. It was obvious that marriage wasn't meant to be."

"Well, that's water under the bridge."

"But our friendship doesn't have to be."

God, it was pitiful, hearing Arlianna plead. "Sit back down. We're not done here. You bring me Jessica, complete this match, and Renn remains unharmed. I see he is still in Jessica's time." Natasha tapped her screen. "I assume you fired him."

"I did."

Natasha kept her eyes on Arlianna. Not one single blink from her ex-friend. Arlianna really was good at hiding her emotions.

Too bad Natasha was going to have to fire her, too, once this fiasco was over. Then see how the most famous of all matchmakers dealt with her future. But by then Natasha's position in the company would once again be secure.

"That's good. No one wants a half-assed apprentice, now do they?" Natasha leaned back, crossing her arms over her chest. "Once the girl has been transported to Frank, cammed and established, you will have a new apprentice and we can resume activity as normal."

"And I have your word about Renn?" Arlianna asked.

"He can do whatever he pleases, as long as he stays out of my way," Natasha lied. Of course, Renn couldn't be allowed to come back and destroy her reputation.

"I'll make sure of that. I can set him up at the museum," Arlianna said, tucking her curly hair behind her ears. "And I'll get Jessica."

"Good."

Arlianna's obligation now included camming Jessica. When it came to matchmaking, Arlianna was known for always following the rules. This would keep her out of the way while Natasha went after Renn.

"Are we done here?" Arlianna stood up.

"We're done. For now." Natasha turned on her holocom. "I'll be watching you."

"I'm sure you will." Arlianna smiled. "And I'll be watching you."

For one split second Natasha remembered how they used to laugh together as small girls. Bait each other and play silly games. But this one wasn't silly. Her future depended on its outcome.

Pushing her memories aside, Natasha turned to her screen. Renn's data showed several visits to 1987. Whatever was that fool doing?

Chapter Twenty-Four

Renn stood outside Jessica's door, his hand poised for knocking, when a branch brushed against his neck.

Turning around, he faced the tiny yard. And damn if he didn't hear a soft voice weaving between the leaves.

Be kind to her.

A large branch bent down, nearly scraping his face and then rose up again.

This booting through time was messing with his mind. It had to be that. Trees did not talk. Not in this time. Not in his time. Only in Fairytale time.

He took a few deep breaths, stabilizing his core.

Be kind. The words whispered behind him. His neck tickled. *Be honest.*

It would be easy to appear in Jessica's room. But instead, he knocked. When she didn't answer, he knocked again.

He shifted his feet, willing her to answer. This way of communicating was not easy. But if he wanted to make this work, he was going to have to act like a normal person. One of the most normal traits of this time was carrying around a cellphone, which he didn't own.

After knocking again, he gave up.

The tree swayed gently against his forehead as he turned around and walked away.

****

"Jessie."

"Grandpa?" My eyes shot open. A drill worked its way through my chest. "Is something wrong with Grandma?" I threw my legs over the side of the bed.

In the three years since I'd lived in this apartment, my grandfather has only been inside one time. And that was to show the plumber my bathroom which needed unclogging. I was sure something was terribly wrong.

"No, no, honey." He patted my arm. "She's fine. That fella in the coat is here."

"Here?" I looked around, knowing Renn could appear anywhere, anytime. My brain was fuzzy from sleep, but my eyes were clear as water. "Where?"

Grandpa nodded toward the main house. "He's a nice fella."

God only knew what my grandmother was saying to him. I threw off my covers and stood up. I heard voices coming from my grandparents' kitchen.

I saw Renn's back when Grandpa opened the connecting door, leaving me to get ready.

I slammed it shut and hurriedly put on the jeans I'd left on the floor last night and grabbed a sweatshirt off my chair. Nothing could be done about my hair. I ran my fingers through the curls and let it fall wherever it wanted.

"Hi," I said, walking into my grandparents' kitchen.

"Good morning, Jessica." My heart jumped at the sound of Renn's rich voice.

He turned away from me and back toward my grandmother. "Not far from here," he said, running his finger over a spot on the table.

God only knew what question elicited that answer.

Realizing my grandmother had a monopoly on his attention, I sat down next to Renn, hoping to stop the interrogation.

"Do you want some coffee?" Grandma asked me. "I couldn't get your friend here to take a cup. Are you sure I can't get you something?"

"No thanks, ma'am," he said. "I had breakfast before I came over." He began twirling his thumbs.

I wanted to reach over and take his hand but held back.

"There's plenty of eggs and bacon if you want to make your friend breakfast. I've got bills to pay." My grandmother refilled her cup, gave me quick thumbs up, and left us alone in the kitchen.

"How come you're in here?" I asked. "Why didn't you just come back to my place?"

"I knocked, but you didn't hear me."

It was hard to believe I didn't hear him outside my door. After my conversation with Arlianna, I was surprised I slept at all.

"You knocked?"

He leaned forward, cupping my face between his warm, soft hands. "For normalcy."

Was he kidding? There was nothing normal about him, and I doubted there ever would be.

"I know what's happened to you," I said.

His smile told me he wasn't going to believe a word I was going to say. But he was willing to play along.

"I had a piece of your coat, and rubbing it pulled you into a time stream."

"And how have you come to know this?" He ran

his finger below my ear. The sensation overpowered my ability to speak.

He pulled me close, brushing his lips gently against mine. I opened my mouth, so ready for a kiss.

"Arlianna likes you," he whispered. "She felt our connection when she met you."

I pulled back. "If you already know I saw her, why are you pretending you didn't?"

He brushed a hair off my forehead. "I'm sorry, Jessica. This isn't easy for me, either. Wanting you so much and not knowing how to act."

"Can you get the fabric back for me? So I can know when you're coming?"

He shook his head. "No can do. As they say. But if I get a cell phone, I can call you."

I wrapped my arms around him, burying my head in his neck. His lemony scent made my groin tingle.

"Let's get one today," he said.

"First, I have other plans." I took his hand and led him into my apartment.

****

Hours later, satiated from lovemaking, after we had tattooed ourselves onto each other's psyche, we strolled hand in hand through the outdoor mall a few miles from my apartment. Renn had assured me I would be safe because we were together.

As we made our way down the sidewalk toward the Verizon store, I studied Renn's profile. His lips were pressed tightly together. He looked from side to side. I'd read in his handbook that time travelers had heightened senses, and I wondered if he was hearing things beyond my range.

A half dozen kids played on a climbing apparatus.

It caught Renn's attention, and he stopped and stared, twirling his thumbs forward and backward.

"Such a multitude of people in one place," he said.

I was still in awe at the strange way he talked, sometimes dropping letters, using abbreviations and at other times, uncommonly used words. "Don't you have malls?"

"Not like this. We have specialty stores, but mostly we shop on the galaxies."

"Galaxies?" I asked.

"Sites on the web. Clusters of clouds make up systems, and systems sit inside galaxies. It's pretty simple."

"Whatever you say." I pictured what he was saying, but I much preferred live shopping to online, and so I didn't think I'd like those galaxies much.

He flinched and covered his ears as a group of teenage girls, linked together like puzzle pieces, giggled as they rushed past us. He winced again when a mom pushing a stroller nearly bumped into his legs.

Feeling his distress, I led him toward a more secluded area.

By the time we reached the bench, after zigzagging around another group of teenagers and a small yapping dog, I could feel the tension rising from Renn. He stared straight ahead, reminding me of the first time when I'd snuck up behind him at The Mud Hut. I thought he might shimmer. But he didn't.

"Do you want some water?" I asked.

He held up his hand and shook his head.

I sat there, looking at him, biting on the inside of my cheek. His shoulders heaved up and down. His hands twitched on his thighs. It seemed like forever before he finally let out a giant breath of air and looked over at me.

"You're still here," I said.

"Apparently so." He smiled. "I suspect too much uncontrolled time streaming has unbalanced my CORE."

I suggested we eat before dealing with the Verizon store. Buying my current phone had turned into a mini-series event. Galaxy shopping was probably quick and easy, and I didn't want Renn to get annoyed with our way of doing things.

We walked toward a deli at the far end of the mall. Our silence stitched us together. Words weren't necessary.

"Let's run away," I suggested after a few minutes. "We'll go somewhere together until Natasha forgets about us."

Renn smiled, his whole face lighting up. "If only we could."

"Why can't we?" I watched his eyes grow intense. "Can't you take me somewhere? Anywhere in time?"

I was tempted to add that we could go back to when my mother was still alive, but I didn't. And I didn't know why. Maybe because if he said yes, then I would have to seriously consider leaving the life I now had. As it stood, I wanted to be with him forever, but I wanted that forever to be here.

"She'll find us, Jessica. There is no escape. That's why…" He put his arm around my waist, pulling me closer to his side. "Later. We'll talk later."

I hated that word. *Later* was just a step below *but* in the negative news category. David's *postponed* talk involved asking for his ring back. My advisor wanted a proposal from me *later* this month. Mom said we'd talk *later* about my birthday party. That *later* never came.

"You're sad," Renn said.

I gave his shoulder a bump.

"Don't be." He ran a finger across my lips. "We have each other."

I wasn't so sure about that.

"To answer your earlier question about why Natasha picked you. You are creative and compassionate. But you've lost your ambition, and you've been questioning your future. You have strong family ties, and in your quest to know your mother, you've developed the need to be a mother yourself. Traits that make you almost a soulmate for this Frank guy."

I glanced at him as we walked. "Is there anything you don't know about me?"

"I don't know what it's like to kiss you in a mall."

He pulled me toward him and pressed his lips on mine. My insides exploded. Okay, so he had the advantage of knowing more about me than I did about him. But it really didn't matter. I knew the most important thing about him. He was my soulmate. No one in the world could make my insides spin with a kiss the way Renn could.

Chapter Twenty-Five

We followed the hostess to a booth in the back of the deli. I climbed in, expecting Renn to sit opposite me. Instead, he sat down on the same side, taking off his coat and setting it across from us on the bench. The coat took on a life of its own, giving off a soft light that rose up over the table.

"What's your coat made of?" I heard Kyle's suspicious voice in my mind as I asked.

"Cotton and silk," he said. "So, this is a paper menu." He picked up the menu and flipped it over a few times, running his hand over its glossy texture.

I squinted my eyes at him.

"It was mandatory to take Early 21st Century Dining and Meals. And we had samples of these things. With paper being so outrageous, only the most exclusive restaurants still use them. Mostly we order off Emerils and punch in our orders."

I laughed. "My grandpa loves his show."

"Bam!" Renn pointed his finger in the air, imitating Emeril Lagasse. "So, what's good here?" He squeezed my leg, making it hard for me to think about anything but his naked body.

"You." I touched the side of his face, feeling his soft beard. He placed his hand on top of mine. "You know this is torture, don't you?"

His lips moved slightly as he read the menu. "What

do you suggest?"

"They have great steak fries," I said.

"You two ready to order? Our pastrami is the best." Our waitress towered above us. Her blonde hair fell across the side of her face. She tossed the strands out of her eyes with a suggestive smile, obviously meant for Renn.

I moved closer to Renn, pointing my finger at a glossy photo of a hot roast beef sandwich. "That's my favorite."

He placed his finger next to mine.

"Okay, I'll have that," he said, quickly. "You, too?"

"No, I'll have a chopped salad."

He raised his eyebrows at me.

"I don't feel like meat right now." What I really didn't feel like was having beef juice dribble down my chin.

Along with our meals we decided to split an order of fries.

"That's all," I said to the waitress, who didn't seem in any hurry to leave.

"Do I know you?" she asked Renn. "You look so familiar."

Right. Like you're a time traveler, too.

"I don't think so," Renn said, turning to face me.

Getting the hint we were finished ordering, she finally left us alone.

"Do you know her?" I asked.

He bent his head closer to mine and whispered. "I have seen her before. Around 1999. She was about twelve. Arlianna and I were at a park for the 4th of July."

I pressed the side of my cheek against my teeth, listening, trying to imagine what it would be like to time travel.

"And she was…" He stopped talking and gave me a sly smile. "Jessica, I've never seen her before in my life."

I hit him in the chest. "Don't tease me like that. It's not fair. I don't know a thing about you, and you seem to know too much about me."

Our annoying waitress returned with our food and asked Renn, not me, if we needed anything else.

"Some ketchup," I answered.

The waitress returned a minute later with the bottle. She plunked it down in front of Renn, winked at him, and then walked away. I rolled my eyes, shaking my head.

"What do you want to know about me?" Renn picked up his sandwich. "Fire away."

Aunt Beth once told me you learn more about a person by asking unusual questions involving feelings and likes. Did he like having his back rubbed? What was his favorite ice cream, seashell, and song? Did he see shapes in the clouds?

I thought of the questions I answered when creating a fictional character. That process could take weeks, and our time was limited.

"Let me start with some facts," he said, sensing my hesitation. "I'm thirty-three. Four years and five months older than you. I was born on January 24th."

I stuck my fork into a piece of lettuce and carefully put it into my mouth.

"After high school, I attended the local CC, like everyone else. Then went to United States U. My goal was to work at the History Museum. But there weren't any openings, and I had a huge debt. Arlianna found me, pondering my future over a bowl of chicken soup, and said I was perfect for matchmaking."

I kept chewing, tasting nothing.

"This is my first solo mission. One more, and I would have graduated from apprentice to a Level One Matchmaker." He raised his shoulders and lowered them while exhaling.

"You sound disappointed."

"Apprehensive," he said.

I picked up a fry and moved it around in the ketchup, making a circular design.

"What else do you want to know?" he asked.

"How do you time travel?"

"With that." He nodded across the table toward his coat. "It bends the time/space continuum."

The fabric seemed to move as Renn talked.

"How does it actually work?"

"I don't know exactly. By some type of electrical current." He took a bite of his sandwich. "You're right. This beef is the tops."

"You're changing the subject. Can everyone time travel?"

"Not everyone. Those with high electromagnetic fields can't travel at all, and those of us with RH neg blood find it really easy."

"RH negative blood?" I put my arm on Renn's.

He wiped his mouth with his napkin, nodding his head.

"I'm RH negative," I said.

"I know. That's why it's easy for Natasha to manipulate you."

A shadow fell across our table. Our flirty waitress was back. "Are you two doing okay?"

Her lips moved, but no words came out. Not for a few seconds after she stopped talking.

I turned quickly to Renn, watching him as he answered her.

"We're fine," he said. His lips and voice were in perfect sync.

"How about more water?" The waitress filled our glasses.

I heard the water slosh into my glass several seconds after it left the pitcher.

I grabbed onto Renn's hand. "It's happening again."

Renn put his fingers on my pulse, his lips moving slightly as he counted.

"Like in the hospital. Everything is off." The voices around me grew louder until I could hear distinct conversations coming from every table. I put my hands over my ears.

Renn's body stiffened. "Natasha's here. Outside the restaurant."

"Oh. Ugh. Please." I could barely talk. I squeezed Renn's arm.

"Yes, her energy is flowing toward you."

In my peripheral vision, I saw his coat lift several inches off the chair and then settle back down. I closed my eyes and leaned my head into Renn's shoulder. His heart beat fast and hard against my arm. His breathing came heavy and deep.

Renn wrapped his arm around me. "Breathe. Slowly. It's going to be okay."

The voices around me subsided. I dared to open my

eyes. I watched the man at the next table talking to his wife. His words were almost in sync with his mouth. Almost.

I buried my head in Renn's chest again, until I heard the busboy taking away our plates. Again, I peeked, praying everything would be normal. The sound of the dishes stacking on top of each other was in complete sync with the boy's hands as he piled the plates. It was the sweetest sound I'd heard all day.

"She's gone," he whispered.

"I know."

"But she will be back."

I knew that, too.

I lifted my head, exhaled, and leaned back against the seat.

"This has been happening to me ever since I left the hospital. Every time Natasha is nearby. You know what that means, don't you?" I didn't wait for him to answer. "I can leave my house, and I'll always know if she's around."

"Unacceptable. She's too quick for you," Renn said.

"I have a plan. You just said that people with high-energy fields can't time travel. And I know that from your laws."

He gave me a perplexed look.

"I have your old disc, remember?" I went on before he could say anything. "And Kyle has that condition. I'm sure of it. His body emanates all the time. You saw the weird shoes he wears. All I have to do is hold onto him."

"What are you getting at?"

"He can ground me."

"He'd do that for you?" Renn asked. "I know how he feels about me."

"He doesn't trust you. But we're good friends. And yes, I know he'd do it for me."

"I'm not sure it will work," Renn said.

"It's your law. Number 25."

"Laws written by Natasha."

"You said yourself. People with high electromagnetic fields can't time travel."

"In our time," Renn said. "I have no idea what it's like here. This smells like a bad idea."

"Well, I'm sorry." I picked up my purse. "I won't be a prisoner in my house. It's the only way. And for that matter, it helps you, too. I can warn you when she's around. Now, if you'll let me out, I have to use the bathroom." I shoved my shoulder against his.

"I read that you were stubborn," Renn said, without moving.

"I'm just being practical."

Renn ran his finger down the side of my face. Desire pulsated throughout my body. I wanted him more than anything in the world.

"I just want you to be safe while I'm…"

"Gone?" I interrupted.

"She can't go on making false matches. Disturbing true soulmates." Renn picked up his water glass, then set it back down without taking a sip. "She has to be called out in public. You know that as well as I do."

"Let me out." I pushed against him. "Move."

Reluctantly, he stood up and let me out of the booth. As I walked toward the bathroom, he grabbed my hand.

"I'm coming with you."

"Not into the bathroom, you're not."

"I'll stay outside the door."

I hurried across the deli with Renn on my heels. Once inside the stall, I called Lilly. No answer. I sent her a text. *—B at my house at 6.—*

The minute I opened the bathroom door, Renn took my hand. He offered to buy lunch, but all he had was a hundred-dollar bill. I used the credit card I carried for emergencies. What bigger emergency than knowing your soulmate was leaving, possibly forever?

"You do understand that I have to leave, don't you, Jessica?" Renn said as we approached my car.

The pressure against my chest made it difficult to breathe. I wanted nothing more than to hold him tightly, to feel his burning skin against mine.

"Let me have the keys." Renn held out his hand. "You're too upset to drive."

"I am not." I stood in front of the driver's door, angry tears rolling down my cheeks.

"Oh, for crap's sake, Jessica. Do you think this is easy for me? I don't want to go. I don't want you to spend all your time with some other guy. But that's what you're going to do. And I need to see that Natasha gets her just punishment. Now give me the keys."

I squeezed my eyes shut, trying to stop the tears, but it was no use. He rubbed his finger across the tender skin beneath my eye.

"Let's not make this harder than it has to be." He kissed me gently on the lips, then backed away.

He held his hand out again. I gave in and climbed into the passenger seat. He pushed the driver's seat back giving his long legs room to stretch.

"What?" I asked.

"You look even more beautiful when you're upset."

I tried not to smile, but I couldn't help myself. "Just drive."

"Start engine. Forward, merge into traffic." He patted the dashboard. Then reached around under the console.

"What are you doing?" I asked.

He tossed his head back, chuckling. "Forgetting that I'm not at home. See what you do to me? Our cars are DVA. Oh, sorry. Driverless, voice-activated."

"Of course, they are. Have you ever actually driven?" Last thing I wanted now was to get into a car accident.

"Assimilated driving."

"Don't tell me. One of your mandatory classes."

"How did you guess? Just watch me."

Renn eased the car gently from the curb and cruised slowly down the block. I wasn't sure which one of us was the most nervous.

"I won't be gone long," he said.

"You can't make that promise." I glanced at his profile. His nostrils flared slightly.

He revved the engine and sped off down the street. During the rest of the drive, our unspoken words sat between us like an unwanted passenger.

****

Lilly sat on my front steps with her hands tucked between her legs. She stood up as Renn jerked the car to a stop.

"Thank God, we made it home," I said.

Renn smirked, opened his door, slammed it shut, and rushed around to open mine. I tensed as he helped me out. I hated him for wanting to leave, and I hated myself for wanting him so much.

"Hi, I'm Lilly." She threw her arms around Renn. If he was surprised at her affectionate greeting, he kept it to himself. Something he probably learned in one of his crazy classes.

"Nice to meet you," Renn said.

"C'mon in." Lilly looped her arm through Renn's.

Renn glanced at me. "Not now. I have some business that needs attending to."

"Oh, okay then." Lilly tilted her head at me. I could tell she knew something was wrong.

"I hope I see you again, soon. I'll meet you inside, Jess."

I ached for Renn to tell me he changed his mind. That he wasn't going to leave. But he didn't. He put his hands on my shoulders.

"When will I see you again?" I asked.

"Soon." Then he kissed me in that delicious way, his beard tickling my cheek.

He left me standing on the porch, with my hands pressed to my lips. My list of words I hated was getting longer.

Once inside, I fell against the closed door and slid to the floor. Tears poured out of me in fast forward motion. Covering my hands, I rocked back and forth.

Lilly sat down next to me, rubbing my back.

"He's leaving," I choked out.

"I'm so sorry."

"I have to get Kyle to help me." I wiped my nose with the back of my hand. "Until Renn comes back. If he comes back."

"You know he will."

"I'm not so sure."

"I am. I saw the way he looks at you," Lilly said. "And that kiss."

"You were spying on us?"

Lilly smiled.

"Of course, you were." I smiled, too. "It's all too insane."

I found a tissue in my purse and blew my nose before telling her how Kyle's condition, even though it sounded ridiculous, could save my life.

Lilly listened, all the while nodding and throwing in an occasional uh huh. When I was finished, she pulled my phone out of my purse and handed it to me. "Call him now."

Natasha's image barged into my mind. I punched in Kyle's number, taking deep breaths to slow my heart down.

****

The full moon cast a circle of light on the ocean. From his motel porch, Renn watched the waves roll in, flatten, and roll back out. The motion was mesmerizing, but it couldn't rid him of the physical ache sitting in the pit of his stomach. He'd read about the tortuous knots that developed in one's insides, but he never believed it to be true, merely the flowing words of the romance writers he had studied. Now he knew it could be worse.

He had left her uncertain of his return. With that crazy idea of having her friend, Kyle, keep her safe. Thinking of them together pained him, but he had acted to the contrary. He had acted like a fool. As if he didn't give a damn. When that's all he did give. A lone star twinkled in the sky.

It was the sign he needed to move forward.

Natasha must be stopped.

But he had to see Jessica one last time before going home.

Instant communication

To Natasha from Renn - Working on my own now. Arlianna not responsible for my actions.

Repeat: NOT responsible.

Chapter Twenty-Six

I thought about Renn all night. All through my grandmother's meatloaf dinner. Through watching *Sex and the City* reruns with Lilly. Especially through the conversation I had with Kyle when he returned my call around ten-thirty, as I was getting into bed.

"Hey," he said. "What's up?"

"Not much. Where are you?"

"Doing clean up. I'm closing all week. Management decided that a guy has to be here at night."

"Makes sense," I said.

"I still don't see your name on the schedule."

"I'm on leave. For the next few weeks, at least." I heard rushing water in the background.

"Gives you time to write."

"True." I ran my finger along a crack in the wall. "Are you working tomorrow? We need to talk."

"You've come to your senses about Renn, and you need me to coach you through the dark times?"

"No." I chuckled. "But I do need your help. Can we meet tomorrow?"

"I've got a client after my shift. I can meet you here afterward. You want to meet at the new wine bar across the street?"

More than anything, I wanted to say yes. I'd join him, like old times. But this was a new time, and I had a threat hanging over my head, as strange as it may be.

"How about here?" I asked, raising my voice a little.

"A little us time?"

"Kyle, we already tried that." I kept my voice light and breezy, pushing away the anxiety reeling through my body.

We arranged to meet after his shift tomorrow. No matter how much Kyle thought he knew what was bothering me, he'd never guess in a million years what I was going to ask him.

I tossed my phone onto my nightstand next to the leaves Renn had plucked from my tree. The disc, almost completely blank, was safe inside my nightstand drawer.

With a renewed energy, I opened my journal.

His presence moved her to places she had only imagined. Touching him became a part of what made her who she was.

The darkness unfolded exposing another layer of evil. Without someone to destroy, there was no one left but herself.

What started off as random thoughts became connected in ways I never imagined. Closing the journal, I was filled with lightness. I could feel the spaces between each word breathing life to the story.

It was time to send something to my advisor.

****

The next morning, I woke up with the urge to spend time with my grandparents. I'd been avoiding them. But after last night's surge of writing I felt more positive than I had in days.

I put on a pair of sweatpants and a T-shirt and

walked into their kitchen.

Something wasn't right.

An eerie silence met me as I crossed the cold tile. I didn't hear my grandfather snoring from his living room chair or the clicking of computer keys from my grandmother's office.

Not seeing a note from Grandma heightened my uneasiness.

The newspaper was still in its plastic wrapper. A glass with a few drops of orange juice sat on the table next to a cup of cold coffee.

I walked slowly down the hallway to my grandparents' bedroom, feeling the silence that lay ahead. Each breath stopped in my chest for a second before it came out.

Panic swelled inside me.

"Get a grip," I whispered. My senses were in sync. Natasha was not here. At least, that's what I kept telling myself. She. Was. Not. Here. And apparently neither were my grandparents.

I turned off the dripping faucet in their bathroom, left their room, and headed back toward the kitchen. My step was lighter. But when I called my grandmother's cell and heard it ringing in the living room, my heart sped up again. Trying to remain calm and act normal, I poured myself a cup of coffee and sat down at the table, unwrapping the newspaper. I read the headlines, but I was merely reciting the words in my head without grasping their meaning.

The seconds turned into minutes. The clock chimed. The refrigerator hummed.

As I began to relax the world shifted slightly. I heard footsteps behind me. My breath escaped into the air like thin wisps of snow. My body shook from the inside out.

I grabbed my grandmother's letter opener off the counter, raised it in the air, and spun around. A tall man stood in front of me.

"Jessie, honey."

"Papa!" My body sagged. "What are you doing here?"

"I didn't mean to scare you."

I flung my arms around my father. His large belt buckle poked against my stomach as I hugged him tighter. He smelled just like he was supposed to. A mixture of mint aftershave and cherry pops. I didn't realize how much I had missed him until he squeezed me back, making up for all the hugs we'd missed in the last few months.

"How's my little cowgirl?"

I pulled away and stared at him. He took off his black leather hat and set it brim up on the table.

His bushy eyebrows, hanging over his glasses, still reminded me of tufts of grass. But his hairline had receded several inches since his last visit. What little hair he had left was almost all grey.

He was thinner and more muscular. Most likely due to his current role. As always, he wore a plaid shirt, jeans, and cowboy boots.

"Why are looking at me like that?" Pa asked. "I don't look that different, do I? Well, my ponytail's a smidge longer."

His words were in total sync with his lips. I had been freaking out over nothing.

"I'm just glad to see you. I mean, really glad."

The front door opened, and I heard my

grandparents coming toward the kitchen.

"Hey there, Jake." Grandpa gave my dad a loose hug, his eyes brimming with tears. "Good to see you. Your flight was okay?"

"Smooth sailing. I can't say the same for that whipper-snapper who drove me here," Pa answered.

Grandma came in a second later, carrying a large grocery bag. She set the food on the table next to my dad's hat and squeezed him tightly. Her head barely came up to his shoulder.

"I'm sorry, Jessie," she said. "I forgot to leave a note."

Not as sorry as I was. "No worries."

"Are you surprised?" Grandpa asked me.

"Why didn't you tell me he was coming?"

"It was my idea to keep it all hush-hush," Pa said.

"We rushed off so fast in order to get back here before your dad." Grandma placed canned vegetables and pasta into the cupboard. "But I guess we weren't quick enough. Have you had breakfast?"

"Not yet." I ran my fingers around the brim of my dad's hat. His presence made our house feel complete.

"Your hands are shaking," Grandma said. She clasped my hands between hers and massaged my fingers. "And they're so cold. I'll turn up the heat."

"It's not too cold," I lied. "Papa, are you hungry? I'll make that omelet you like so much. We have peppers, don't we, Grandma?"

I needed something to keep me busy. Anything.

"I'm not hungry, little lady," Pa said. "How about just a cup of Joe."

"You got it." All my life I'd been embarrassed by my father's old-fashioned language. But right now, I could speak cowboy talk all day, I had missed him so much.

"You two need some time alone," my grandmother said. She excused herself to pay bills insisting my grandfather meet her in their office.

"So, how is life treating you?" Pa asked, taking a sip of his coffee. "You seem a bit off your saddle. Are you expecting someone? You keep looking outside."

"No." I smiled, savoring his words. A sparrow skimmed by the window. "How long are you here for? I thought the shoot didn't end until August."

"Eh? My part was basically over," he said, squinting at me. "You look fine as a daisy. I was expecting you to…"

"Aunt Beth called you, didn't she?" I interrupted.

If anyone told the truth, it was my dad. He never even told those little white lies my grandmother insists are okay in order to not hurt someone's feelings.

"She was worried about you."

"What'd she tell you?" I asked.

"You know your aunt. She said you were hospitalized and almost kicked the bucket."

I snickered. "As you can see, I'm fine. And I did not almost die."

But when he gave me a concerned look, where he presses his lips together, puts his fingers on his chin and sort of smiles, I lost my composure. Tears streaked my face because my family was safe and because I was so scared about what was happening to me.

"Come here." He held open his arms. We hugged for several minutes. That's all it took, and I felt a million times better. At least for the moment.

"Tell me what's going on?" he said.

"It's crazy. You won't believe me."

"We all got pieces of crazy in us, some bigger pieces than others. How about we talk outside?"

This was a pretty big chunk of crazy I was about to tell him.

My father opened the umbrella on the picnic table to keep the sun out of our eyes. For the next hour, we sat and talked. Well, I talked. Pa mostly listened with an occasional uh huh, his bushy eyebrows curved inward, the way they used to get when I told him stories as a little kid.

"That's quite a tall tale," he said when I was through. "Good to see you haven't lost your imagination."

"You don't believe one word, do you?"

"Jessie." He lowered his head, peeking over the top of his glasses. "Did you expect me to?"

I shrugged. "I guess not."

"You've been under a lot of pressure, from what your grandmother tells me. School. Your breakup. Car problems. Which, you should have come to me about."

"But Pa, I saw him disappear," I said. "Several times."

"I believe that you believe you saw him go poof." He raised his hands in the air. "But, hey, you know about special effects, what with your uncle in the business."

"Then I must be losing my mind."

"Oh, for Pete's sake, Jessie. There's nothing wrong with you. Besides you're too young to be in love." He took two cherry pops out of his pocket and handed me one.

"Too young? I'm twenty-nine. Most of my friends

are married. With careers and futures. You were already married to Mom by then. And what about that woman who's after me?"

"Now listen here." Pa stuck the pop in the corner of his mouth. "I haven't been the best father. I know that. But I'm here now. And no one is going to take you anywhere. Besides, time travel is pure hog wash."

"You don't know that." I unwrapped the cherry pop, even though I didn't really want it. The sweet flavor exploded into my mouth.

"I know you've been through something traumatic and that…"

"No," I said, getting up. "You're wrong."

"Hey, there you are." Renn walked through the side gate, his hands in the pockets of his trench coat.

"Renn!" I jumped out of my chair. "I thought you left."

"I couldn't leave without seeing you again."

I threw my arms around him, inhaling his lemony scent. I could feel his heartbeat against the crook of my neck. "Come meet my father."

Taking his hand, I pulled him toward the picnic table. We had only taken a few steps when Renn stopped walking. His hand tensed in mine as he stared at my father.

It's not often that people recognize my pa since most of his movies are European spaghetti westerns. But every now and then someone does.

"Pa, this is Renn. Renn, meet my pa, Jacob."

"Glad to make your acquaintance, son." He stood up, extending his hand.

Those old feelings of wishing he were more normal rose to the surface.

Renn stood stiff as a mannequin, gawking, his arms at his sides. Sure, my pa was weird, but Renn was really overreacting. I nudged him with my elbow bringing him back from wherever he had gone.

"Nice to meet you too, sir," Renn said, his voice faltering. "A real pleasure."

"Jessie's told me about you," Pa went on, giving Renn the once-over.

"She has?" Renn gave me a quizzical look.

"Oh, all good, I assure you. Please sit down." Pa motioned to the empty chair.

I pulled my chair closer to Renn's and placed my hand on his armrest.

"So, tell me young man, you live around here?"

I groaned inside. It was a typical father to boyfriend question, but Renn wasn't your typical guy.

"Not far," Renn said.

Only over one hundred years from now, I wanted to add. But I kept silent.

"And you're about thirty?"

"Thirty-three, sir."

"What do you do for a living?"

"Papa." I finally entered the conversation. "Please, don't give him the third degree. I'm not a teenager anymore."

"It's okay, Jessica." Renn smiled at me. His uneasiness passed replaced by a regular guy who knew perfectly well how to handle my father. "I work for an internet-based company."

All true there.

"An established one, I hope." Pa pulled a cherry pop from his pocket. "Have a hankering for one?"

"Thanks." Renn took the sucker but didn't remove

the wrapper.

"They're sweet, but good," I said.

"Don't force the young man, if he doesn't want one," Pa said. "So, tell me, what goods do you sell?"

"We're in the service business, sir." Renn twirled the stick between his fingers.

Still true.

"How so?" Pa asked.

"Mind if I ask you a question?" Renn leaned back, crossing his arms in front of his chest.

"Shoot."

"Where is your family from?"

Pa straightened up in his chair. "Jessie hasn't told you?"

"No, sir."

"We haven't known each other that long," I said.

The story of my father's unusual past, of how he couldn't remember anything from before his life with my mom didn't usually come up in casual conversation. Fact is, he rarely talked about it anymore. None of us did.

"My father had some kind of accident right before he met my mom, and he's never been able to remember anything," I said. "But it's been okay. He became part of my mom's family, and that's all that mattered."

Renn's face took on a reverent look.

"But I'm sure you know where you're from, young man," Pa said, not even trying to hide the sarcasm in his voice.

Renn nodded. "Just north of here."

"And this business you're in, you makin' good dough?"

"Pretty much so." Renn reached over and squeezed

my hand.

The situation was about as comfortable as wearing one of those white paper gowns, waiting for the doctor. Pa glanced from me to Renn and back to me again.

"Aren't you tired?" I asked my father.

"I should be. But I get your drift." He grinned at Renn. "I'll leave you two alone."

Renn stood up. "It's been an honor."

An honor? Being polite is one thing, but that was carrying it a bit too far.

Pa squeezed my shoulder as he walked past my chair.

We waited until he was inside before moving to a lounge. Renn's coat felt soft against my arms.

Without saying anything I kissed him as if I hadn't seen him in years. As our tongues pressed together, the heat spread from between my legs up through my entire body. I craved his nakedness against mine.

Renn shifted in the lounge, pulling me on top of him. If not for the fact that my grandparents and my dad were in the house, we would have made love right there in the backyard.

"I was so worried about you," he said between kisses.

"Tell me you're here to stay." I danced my fingers over his chest, twirling a soft, blond hair with the tip of my pinky.

"I'm under strict orders to quietly disappear."

"Renn." His name escaped softly from my lips. I wasn't even sure I had said anything. "Are you?"

He held my face between his hands. "You must not take chances while I'm gone."

"Is that why you came back? To lecture me about

my life? Weren't you listening when I told you about Kyle?"

"You're going through with that?" he asked.

I rolled onto my side. "I can't just sit around doing nothing. If I can't come with you. At least with Kyle I'll be safe."

"Maybe." Renn shook his head.

"And what was it with my father? You acted so strange when you saw him. Telling him it was an honor meeting him? Please, don't tell me they taught you that in one of your classes. Because it's a bit overboard."

"We did learn to be polite. But that's not exactly what happened here. I have something to tell you about your mother and father."

Renn glanced toward the house. All the sparkle drained from his eyes. He sucked on his lower lip, taking a deep breath.

I untangled myself from his limbs and sat up at the foot of the lounge.

"Did you see my mom on one of your time travels?" That pressure against my chest, the one that made it hard to breathe, crept up on me.

Renn put his arms around me and pulled me close. I inhaled his sexiness, wishing so much he was just a normal guy who I could count on for the rest of my life.

"I believe so," he said. "But what's more important is what I'm going to tell you."

I picked at a tear in the lounge. "What could be more important than my mom?"

"To you, probably nothing. But to us in the future, your parents are famous. And seeing your father's face jolted my reality. Up until now, I've only seen it in our *Big Book of Success Stories.*"

His words scared me. Did I want him so badly I fell for his crazy time traveling story?

"Your father and mother are one of our most successful matches to date. They truly were soulmates. Your father was picked up by one of our first matchmakers in 1872 and brought to your mom in…"

"You're saying my dad is from 1872?" I seriously needed my head checked for ever believing him.

Renn placed his fingers over my lips. "Yes. Think about it, Jessica. He doesn't remember anything from before meeting your mom. I know their entire history. He was picked up by one of our best matchmakers, Sienna, and taken to Arezzo where your mom was traveling. And I guarantee you he has very vivid dreams about his past."

I studied Renn's jawline as the words sank into my brain. All my life, my dad's been telling me about this one recurring dream of his. About a ranch with a gigantic room and a covered wagon with one broken wheel. Maybe Renn was telling the truth.

"And furthermore," Renn continued. "As a child of matched parents, if you haven't found your soulmate by the age of twenty-three, your odds decrease significantly. That's probably the biggest reason Natasha picked you for Frank."

He ran his thumb down my jawline, sending a river of warmth through my body. I placed my hand on his, staring into the blueness of his eyes. "I…I…This is so…" My lips parted against his.

Neither of us heard my grandmother until she was standing a few feet away from us.

"Kyle is here," she said.

"Can you talk to him for a few minutes?" I asked.

"Keep him inside."

"I'll try." Her eyes crinkled as she nodded at me and headed back toward the house. "But you know Kyle."

"I should be going anyway," Renn said. "I came to tell you I do care about you touching Kyle. It does hurt to think about. I want you to know that. You must believe me."

"I want to," I said.

I leaned forward to kiss him when Kyle came through the sliding door, ignoring my grandmother as she tried to stop him. One glance at Renn and the smile on his face disappeared. His eyes narrowed into a glare, directed at Renn.

I rushed toward Kyle, stopping him from getting any closer.

"What is he doing here?" he asked.

"Chill." Renn raised his hands in the air. "Everything's good."

Kyle's body tensed. He clenched and unclenched his fists, anger spreading onto his face.

"Relax," Renn said. "I was just leaving."

"You bet you are." Kyle stepped forward. "I don't know who you think you are hanging around her, after what you did."

"He didn't do anything." I grabbed Kyle's arm. The size of the shock passing between us startled me. I flinched and jumped back.

"Is that what you were talking about with his extra energy?" Renn asked.

"You guys were talking about me?" Kyle said.

I stood between them, feeling as if I were balancing on a tightrope.

"Jessica has this idea that..." Renn started.

"Let me tell him." I took Renn's hand and pulled him toward the side gate. "I have to do this my way," I whispered.

I leaned forward, stopping anything he might have said with a long, luscious kiss. My groin ached for his touch. I wanted his tongue against the inside of my thigh. Sliding down my legs. Over my belly. I wanted this kiss to never end.

Renn pulled away first. He cupped my face in his hands. "I love you." His word brushed against my lips like a soft feather.

"I love you, too."

With his hand on the gate, Renn turned to face Kyle.

"Keep her safe," he said.

The sleeves of Renn's coat shimmered as he waved. My heart twisted and tugged. I wanted to throw myself in his arms again.

The gate clicked shut, with my soulmate on the wrong side. With me standing helpless, wondering when I would see him again. If ever.

****

Renn walked quickly down the block. The image of Jessica's fists pressed against each other as he backed out of her yard chiseled a hole in his already breaking heart.

Fortunately, Natasha's plan had failed. He couldn't bear to think of another man kissing Jessica's delicious lips, holding her curvy body, pressing against her.

Oh crap. He had to stop thinking of her. And focus on the task in front of him—bringing Natasha to justice.

He didn't know if Frank Griffin was still waiting

for his soulmate, but he was going to make sure Frank was informed of Natasha's felony behavior.

He realized he had stopped walking and picked up his pace. But no matter how fast he moved, Jessica's image stayed with him.

After meeting Jessica's father, it was all beginning to fall into place.

When Jessica touched the fabric in his presence he was booted to her parents' wedding. Her touch had spun him to her beginning, another proof that they were soulmates. Several years after that wedding day, she'd been conceived. She was at that beach in spirit, in the love her parents shared.

If it all worked out as he wanted, once Natasha was behind bars, maybe they could travel together to meet her mother.

He sent a message to Arlianna.

Mission #265

Instant Communication

Renn: I have news about Jessica's father

Arlianna: Leave it B

Renn: Where R U

Arlianna: Abandon mission ASAP. U R no longer employed. Ret hme

Renn: Abandonment complete.

He touched his locator and spun home.

Chapter Twenty-Seven

From behind her bar Natasha gazed out the picture window of her penthouse. Flowers in every color imaginable created a circular maze bordered by tall, elegant trees.

"It's a beautiful view," Arlianna said. "I see you still have a green thumb."

"It is, isn't it?" Natasha picked up a holo-mote, pressed a button, and the view changed to the ocean, which lay on the other side of the building. "Red or white?"

"Whatever you're having." Arlianna leaned back against the couch, resting her hands on her lap. But Natasha knew she was far from relaxed. Not Arlianna. Her guard never went to sleep.

Slowly and deliberately, Natasha searched through the dozens of bottles on her wine rack. Finally, she settled on a Merlot. She filled two glasses, walked across the room, and handed one to Arlianna.

"You still have these?" Arlianna held the glass up in the air, her eyes on the logo.

"Only that one. The one with my initials. Yours broke years ago."

"Accidentally?" Arlianna asked.

"Shall we say, accidentally on purpose." Natasha sank onto her plush white couch, facing Arlianna.

"It doesn't have to be like this." Arlianna set the

glass down, untouched. "You turn yourself in. I'll guarantee you probation. Tell them the miscalc was accidental. Renn will go on hiatus until it clears over. And then afterward they can live happily ever."

"You expect me to believe you?" Natasha asked. She'd trusted Arlianna one too many times.

"I expect you do the decent thing. The right thing." Arlianna swept a stray hair off her forehead. "Nat, this isn't like you."

"You don't know me anymore." Natasha swirled her glass, watching the wine move counterclockwise and then back in the other direction.

"I know you have a soul inside you. Somewhere."

"I don't want to hurt you, Arl. That was never my intention. But I can't go on trial. And you can't promise me anything." She gave Arlianna a second to deny her accusation before going on. "But I can promise that if you leave it to me, I won't hurt the girl. I'll simply get rid of Renn. As for the mission, I'll report an error in the calcs."

Arlianna shook her head. "I can't have you harming my apprentice."

Natasha's eyes locked onto Arlianna's. A stare down. A game they played when they were kids. But now they were two older women. And Natasha was done playing games.

Natasha took a sip of her wine. "Ah, delicious." She closed her eyes and sighed. "Then I guess we're at an impasse."

She stood up and walked over to the bar. Pressing the holocom, the face of Lexi appeared in the room. "Show our guest out."

"Natasha, please." Arlianna got up and walked to

the bar. Her tattoo shifted into a flower.

"Begging is so unbecoming of you." Natasha refilled her glass.

"I'm not begging. I'm asking. We've all made mistakes."

"The only one I ever made was trusting you. You were never really my friend."

"That's not true." Arlianna reached for Natasha's arm, but Natasha was quick. She grabbed Arlianna, twisting her, holding her in a tight grip.

"I can't be defaced. No one, you hear me, no one is ever going to know about this. Now get out of here." She shoved Arlianna toward Lexi who stood by the door.

"Please, let's work this out. I don't want to hurt you, either. But if I have to…"

Natasha chuckled. "You would."

"Be reasonable."

"Of course. What other way is there to be?"

With that, Natasha picked up the holo-mote, changing the view to the mountains, which lay to the east of the building.

She was going to be reasonable, all right. She would spin Jessica into orbit, sending her from time to time. Renn would follow, of that, she was sure. And if Arlianna got in her way. Well, then, so be it for Arlianna.

Chapter Twenty-Eight

"What did you need to talk about?" Kyle asked. He sat at the picnic table, while I stretched out on the lounge, still feeling Renn's presence. "You know I'll do whatever I can for you."

"Even if it involves Renn?"

Kyle let out mouthful of air. "Against my better judgement."

A breeze whistled through the large tree drooping into our backyard from the neighbor's side of the fence. The branches wrapped long spindly fingers around the telephone wire.

Where to begin? I wanted Kyle to believe me, but it was such an absurd story. Kyle was similar to my dad, a solid guy who only believed in what he could see for himself.

Without giving it any more thought, I blurted out the most important fact.

"Renn is different from us, you're right." I bit on the inside of my cheek and prayed for the best. "He's a time traveler."

Kyle burst out laughing. His cackling carried around the backyard, bringing every bird in a ten-mile radius to the overhead phone wires. "I'm sorry, Jess. Say that again."

"Kyle, I'm serious."

"And I'm from the planet Mars."

An overwhelming feeling of despair washed over me. I needed him to believe me. The tears rose up like champagne foam, bubbling out of me. My shoulders heaved.

Kyle moved over to the end of my lounge. "I'm sorry. I'll listen." He suppressed a smile.

"It is crazy, I know. And I shouldn't love him, but I do. Like you wouldn't believe." I picked at a tear in the lounge chair. "Isn't that what you want? To fall in love so completely? I wanted that with David. And I know you're trying with Heather. But if it's really love, I don't think you have to try. It just is." I wiped the snot off my nose with the back of my hand. "Maybe I just believe him because I want to, but he makes sense."

And then I told him everything. About how the fabric would heat up and how Arlianna stole it from me. The disc. My parents. Natasha. He kept nodding and rolling his eyes. There were jokes waiting to roll off his tongue, but every time he started to talk, I held up a finger. I ended with Law # 25.

"And that's what I need you for."

"There's actually a rule stating high-energy people can't time travel?" A smirk crept onto his face.

I nodded my head "I can't stay inside all the time. Who can possibly do that?"

"Jess. Listen to yourself. It sounds like make-believe. And besides, we've been sitting out here on your porch for over an hour and nothing's happened. And we're not even touching."

The despair I felt grew roots inside my heart. "It's only been a short time. Renn might not even be home yet."

"Call him. You said he has a cell phone now."

"It won't work if he's not in this time." I reached into my pocket for my phone, wishing I still had the fabric. I opened the call icon to my favorites and pressed Renn's name. As I expected, it went to a generic voice stating no message had been set up yet.

"He's gone," I said.

"That doesn't prove he's a time traveler."

I flopped back on the lounge. "It doesn't prove he isn't one, either."

"Now we're talking about the tree in the forest situation," Kyle said. "I vote for it still makes a sound and he's not a time traveler."

My phone dinged, the sound going straight to my heart. But it was Lilly checking in and asking me to come help her pack in the morning.

"We miss you at work," Kyle said.

"I know what you're doing. Changing the subject, talking about small stuff like after David, but this is different."

I closed my eyes. Renn's smile danced behind my eyelids. I felt his lips against mine. His breath on my cheeks. The tenderness of his fingers as he played with my hair. A tear leaked out the corner of my eye.

"Jess." Kyle's voice held the compassion I craved from him. "I can't go everywhere with you, and I doubt Heather will understand. But I'm here for you."

Chapter Twenty-Nine

I called Renn's phone a dozen times during the night. Every time I got the same response: no message has been set up yet. I woke up with a foggy brain. I had plans to hang with Lilly until she left for the airport, but it was way too early to call her. I forced myself to work on my screenplay.

A few hours passed and I was, to my surprise, deep into my writing when Lilly texted.

I dreaded her leaving. Knowing she was close by kept my anxiety at a somewhat manageable level. We'd spent yesterday baking cookies and watching Hallmark movies. Our laughing carried me back to normal days.

After a quick shower and another cup of coffee, I walked outside. My heart pounded in my throat. It was only a dash to Lilly's front door, but time didn't apply to Natasha.

"Morning." I looked up at the tree branches. Her leaves wavered in the sunlight. "Wish me luck."

A branch touched the top of my head as I rushed past her. Lilly's front door was open when I reached it, and I hurried inside.

The minute I saw her open suitcase on her bed, waiting to take her belongings back to London, the flutters started inside me.

"I'm just a text away," Lilly said. "And you have Kyle."

"What if Renn doesn't come back? I mean, seriously, I can't live in fear the rest of my life."

"Any contact from him at all?" Lilly asked as she folded a sweater and set it on her bed along with the rest of her clothes.

"None," I said. "My calls go nowhere."

"Here." Lilly tossed me a sparkly, black tank top, one that I've always loved. "You want this? It doesn't fit me anymore."

I held the top against my chest. "What if he can't get back here?"

Lilly shoved her underwear into the side pocket of her suitcase. "He'll be back. I saw the way he looked at you the other day. And kissed you. Guys don't kiss like that unless they care."

"Not if they put him in jail or whatever they have in the future. I just know he's in trouble. I feel it in my soul."

"Stop obsessing."

I folded her tank top, then unfolded it and folded it again. "I'm trying. I feel like I'm living this other life, not mine."

"Oh, Jessie." Lilly sat next to me on the bed. She put her arm around me, pulling me close to her side. "I wish I could stay. I really do. But I have to get to work. Here, take these, too." She handed me her red high heels. "I never wear them anymore."

"Now I need a dress to go with them," I said.

"Remember that dance in sixth grade? When we wore shoes we couldn't walk in?" Lilly imitated our teetering in those heels.

"We were pitiful," I said. "Life was so uncomplicated. Not like now."

"And we couldn't wait for now," Lilly reminded me.

For the next few hours, we chatted about growing up. Neither one of us wanted to be those awkward kids again. But we also wished life could be as simple. All too soon, her bags were in her mom's car, and we were saying goodbye.

"See you on the porch," she said, giving me a big hug. "At Thanksgiving."

I squeezed her as tight as I could. "I love you."

"I love you, too."

We promised we wouldn't cry. I was having a difficult time keeping true to my words.

"Text me a photo in your new dress. And my shoes," Lilly said, as she got into the car. "Take Renn to some really fancy restaurant."

She was so positive he was coming back. I had to carry her positivity with me, right next to my heart. And then maybe I wouldn't be so unsure.

****

By 8:30 that night, I was mentally exhausted. Stretched out on my bed, I followed the cracks in my ceiling. Their jagged lines disappeared into the corners. When I reached the end, I'd start over again, my eyes roaming back and forth, in a repetitious pattern.

"Jessie." My father stood in the doorway connecting my apartment to the kitchen. He was hunched over, in that way people act when they don't want to intrude.

"I knocked, but you didn't hear me. Your grandmother said I should just come in, but..." He held onto the doorknob.

"It's all right." I sat up, fluffing two pillows behind

my back. "C'mon in."

The mattress sank underneath me as my father sat down. It reminded me of the out-of-syncness I'd felt earlier. And for a split second, my body froze, thinking Natasha was nearby.

"Renn is a good hombre," he said. His words lined up correctly with the movement of his lips. I took a deep breath and relaxed. "Where did he say he lived?"

"Papa don't pretend with me. I told you where he was from."

"I'd like to meet his folks," Pa said.

"I don't know how that's possible." I smoothed my blanket across my lap.

"Jessie, listen up. He obviously cares for you, and I know you care for him. But when dealing with someone slightly off you can't do it with a lick and a promise."

"I don't want to hear any more." I covered my face with a pillow.

My father pulled the pillow away and tossed it to the foot of the bed. "Let me just finish." He pushed his glasses up on his nose. "You need to help him. Not feed his delusions. We really should talk to his family."

"Then what you're saying is that I'm just like him. I'm crazy, too. Because I told you I saw him disappear."

Pa sighed as he reached into his pocket for a cherry pop. He handed me one. I didn't really want it, but I took it anyway and slowly unwrapped the paper.

"No, you're impressionable. You always have been. That's what makes you creative," he said.

"Let me ask you something. Try and be open-minded, okay?" I stuck the pop in my mouth, tucking the sweetness into my cheek. "I know Mom used to believe in all sorts of stuff. I found a bunch of her books on ESP and dreams and channeling people. So, you can't tell me she didn't. She even had one on time traveling. I've still got all of them."

"Your mom, she did have a bit of the frivolous in her. You're like her in those ways."

I just had to blurt it out. "Renn says you and mom were set up by that place he works for. That you came from 1872."

My father stared at me as if I were crazy. "God almighty, Jessie!" He took the cherry pop from his mouth and pointed it at me. "And you believed him?"

"You did have amnesia."

"Can't deny that." He nodded. "That's a mighty far stretch to time traveling."

"But what about those recurring dreams you have about being on a ranch? I was little, but I know Mom wanted to have them analyzed. I remember her saying they must mean something. Renn told me that's what happens when someone is pulled from their time. They dream about it over and over."

"Jessie. Jessie. Jessie." He peered at me over his glasses. "I don't think you should see this fellow anymore."

"That's not going to happen." I hoped. "I know he's my soulmate. Just like you and mom."

"Your mom was something all right." Pa closed his eyes and hummed for a few seconds. I couldn't name the song, but it was what my parents sang to me when I was little.

I knew my father was thinking of my mother. He would watch her fry an egg, or sweep the floor, or sit and read, always with the same dreamy expression on his face. And hum. Just like now.

His singing, his smell of aftershave and cherry, his faraway gaze, it all carried me back to our house with the big front yard and cracked sidewalk.

"Mom was your life, wasn't she?" I asked. "It didn't matter about anything else."

"She sure was. From the moment we met to the day she left us."

"So it could be true, everything Renn told me."

"This isn't one of those movies you watch. This is the real deal."

"And in your real life you work as a cowboy. Why is that? Maybe because that's what you were before. You talk like you came from another century. And with Mom gone, well…you've never been the same after that."

His chest heaved. "Oh, Jessie. I'm sorry for not being around much. I did the best I could."

"Oh, Pa, I know." I leaned forward, putting my arms around him.

"If it wasn't for your grandparents, I don't know what I would have done. I've tried to send you a postcard from every city," he said. "I knew it wasn't much."

"And I love getting them."

"You should be getting one more. I mailed it before getting on the plane."

We snuggled close like we used to when I was a little girl.

"From Arezzo." He said it with a perfect Italian accent, making the Z sound almost like a D. "I hadn't been back there since the day I met your mother. That first time I saw her, standing in front of the fountain, water spraying behind her like mist. Ah, it was love at first sight." He nestled my hair. "I've told you this story a million times, haven't I?"

I smiled. "At least."

"It was like a slice of Heaven dropped into my lap."

"Or maybe you dropped into her life, like Renn said. That's all I'm asking. Just think about it. Mom might even have believed him."

"Strange things do happen. But this story of yours. This is one of the wackiest you've ever told me." He leaned over and kissed me on the forehead. "I better vamoose. Sweet dreams, little lady."

After my father left, I went back to staring at the cracks in the ceiling. Between the lines, I saw my parents' faces. Kissing in front of the kitchen sink. Dancing in the backyard. Laughing as they read the paper.

It all became so clear to me. My screenplay had to be about my parents' love, tragic and beautiful. And how my relationship with Renn mirrored theirs. How Renn and I hoped for the same life together. Finally, I had a direction.

The words came fast and furiously. Pages and pages of scenes. I knew they were out of order, but organization would come later. I would weave what I had written about Renn and me into my parents' love affair.

I'd need my dad's help with the details about how he felt when he arrived here and how it was meeting my mom. Maybe he could remember living in 1892.

But whatever, it was a perfect story for a movie.

I wanted all that perfection with Renn.

Chapter Thirty

I woke up before the sun with my legs tangled in the sheets. I had been dreaming, but all I could remember was being somewhere with Renn and a strong sense of peace. I tried to chase down more of the dream, but it refused to be caught.

Knowing I'd never get back to sleep, I opened my laptop and worked on my proposal. The words came easily and, by the time my apartment was filled with sunlight, I was typing the last sentence. The peaceful feeling from my dream returned to me as I saved the file.

The rest of the next day was a repeat performance of the day before. I hung around the house, helping my grandmother change the bedding and polish her silver. Watched an old western with my dad. Texted Kyle and Lilly. And thought constantly about Renn.

Playing around with his disc was the closest I could come to touching him. But it was almost unreadable Soon, I wouldn't be able to see anything at all.

Law #14 – Upon arrival in new Time, the TTMM must breathe deeply, inhaling particles of current airwaves.

Law # 16 – Do not make attempts at humor. You most likely will be misunderstood.

Law # 18 – Incorporate slang into your dialogue only when you fully comprehend the word's

meaning.

Law # 19 – The transportation of someone other than the subject of a mission is grounds for imprisonment.

It felt like I was reading a science fiction novel. After several hours, I doubted my own sanity.

Later in the afternoon, I knew I'd go crazy if I didn't get outside. Kyle answered my text with a happy face emoji and showed up a half hour later to rescue me from my supposed prison walls.

After discussing our options, we decided to go to The Getty. There was currently an exhibit of modern photography Kyle had been interested in seeing for a while. I didn't really care where I went, as long as I wasn't cooped up in my apartment.

I held onto his arm as I walked to his truck. Once inside, I breathed easier. Most of The Getty Center was indoors, but still, we had to walk through the parking lot to the shuttle bus that took visitors up the hill to the main entrance.

Kyle held my hand the entire way.

It was ridiculous how fast my heart was pounding. My ears felt cloudy, making the voices around us muted. I was lightheaded and unsteady.

I smiled at him. Thankful he wasn't pressing me for small talk.

Once we were inside the main hall, my body sagged with relief. Logically, I knew it was insane to feel like this, to even believe that a woman claiming to be from the future would try to kidnap me. But tell that to my nerves.

Kyle picked up a brochure from the information desk, and together we read the descriptions of today's showings. Other than the photography, there was a Renaissance display and some sculptures. Usually, my favorite part of the Getty was the gardens, but that meant we'd be outside.

I scanned the lobby area.

"I got you." Kyle put his arm around me, pulling me close.

I leaned my head against his shoulder. "I want my old life back."

"No, you don't. Not that shitty one with David. And maybe not one with Renn, either. How about a completely different one?"

He was right. I didn't want those days with David, trying to fit myself into the curves of his life. But I didn't want to live in fear, either. Maybe Kyle was right about Renn. Maybe it would be better if he never came back.

We walked, hand in hand, out the large glass doors toward the next building. The air was still. The sky a pale blue with not a cloud in sight.

"Hungry?" Kyle asked. "Let's get something to eat and sit on the grass."

Please stay indoors. Renn's voice was right there in my head. I tensed up, pressing myself closer to Kyle.

"I told you. I'm here for you," he said.

I knew Kyle was trying to prove how absurd this was. We'd get our food, sit outside, people watch, and it would all be fine.

I agreed to his plan, but I knew I'd stay close to him at all times.

We stood in the cafeteria line behind a mother with two small children. Her little boy wore a long, tan cape. The man in front of her wore a long, tan jacket. Neither resembled Renn's coat. A flower tattoo wrapped around the wrist of the girl preparing the tacos. But of course, it didn't move.

Kyle nudged my arm. "Jess?"

"Huh?" I said.

"Chicken tacos or a salad?"

"Tacos," I said, not really caring.

He carried the tray while I held onto his arm as we found a spot in the shade. I spread out the sweatshirt I had tied around my waist and sat down, making sure my leg touched his.

"I have an idea for my film," I said. "About time traveling."

"Of course, it is. So, this fear of yours," he raised his hand in the air, "will serve some purpose. And you have your uncle for the special effects." Kyle took a bite of his taco, spilling cheese onto his lap.

"I was thinking more of a docudrama. About finding oneself. Breathing in our surroundings until we become one with the world. Missing someone we love, loving someone born in a different time."

The tears welled up inside me. Kyle reached for my hand.

"Hey, doesn't your grandmother always say, what's meant to be is meant to be?"

A shadow fell across our feet.

"So, this is why you want to break it off?" The female voice was not one I expected to hear.

"Heather." Kyle jumped to his feet. I jumped up with him, taking his hand. "What are you doing here?"

"The Renaissance exhibit? Remember, we had mentioned coming here?" She wore a knee length dress with a floral scarf, and comfortable walking shoes. Her hands toyed with the strap of her shoulder bag. Her eyes settled on our hands. I gripped Kyle's so tightly, he couldn't let go.

"We were…"

"Having lunch," I finished for him. "This is not what it looks like. We're just…"

"Friends," Kyle finished for me this time.

"Right," Heather said. "You know, Kyle, I thought you were a decent guy. I guess I was wrong."

She flung her scarf over her shoulder with a huffing sound, turned, and walked away. Kyle shook free of me and hurried after her.

The air behind me shifted. I looked around, searching every face. Near the condiment bar stood a woman in leggings and a lacy black top talking to a man in a suit. The woman's long, red ponytail swung back and forth like a pendulum as she talked. Yet her body wasn't moving at all.

Time became uneven. I hurried to reach Kyle, holding onto his arm again.

"You've gotthisall wrong." I couldn't understand a word he said to Heather. The words came at me after his mouth had closed.

The next minute, his words drawled out, with long pauses. "Weeeee are juuuuuuust friends."

A pain shot through my ears. I leaned closer to Kyle.

Heather was saying something, but the words were way too soft for me to hear. Tears rolled slowly down her cheek. So odd, how I could see the shape of each one.

Her voice rose higher and louder and then she turned away.

Kyle shrugged off my grip. "Heather, wait."

I stumbled trying to catch up to him.

The earth ripped apart. I grabbed at the air as the ground rocked beneath me.

A hand grabbed mine. An icy coldness seeped into my bones. Images of yesterdays flashed past me. My mom dancing down the hallways. My father staring at a photo of my mom, clasping it to his chest, kissing her face. Me, running down the block after a butterfly.

The collage of my life spun faster and faster.

And then everything turned white.

Chapter Thirty-One

My body spun like a dreidel. I thought I would throw up. And then suddenly, it stopped. I was on solid ground.

"Kyle," I said, opening my eyes and reaching out my hand.

My heart hammered against my chest. This. Wasn't. The. Getty. And I was all alone.

I stood in the sand surrounded by palm trees. Lights sparkled off the branches, sending cones of different shades of green onto the ground. A strong salty smell penetrated the air. Seagulls cawed in the distance.

"Kyle!" His name scratched the back of my throat. No matter how loud I screamed, he wouldn't ever hear. He couldn't hear. He was somewhere in another time.

The last thing I remembered was seeing the back of Kyle's head, wavering in the sunlight before I fell onto the museum grass.

I wrapped my arms around my chest, taking deep breaths, willing myself not to freak out. Stay calm. Wasn't that what I had read? **Law #14 - Upon arrival in a new time, breathe deeply, inhaling particles of current airwaves.**

That law applied to a time traveling matchmaker. Not to me. But it was all the arsenal I had. I kept breathing. In and out. Slowly. Stay calm. Breathe. In and out.

Renn had rescued me the last time. He would be here again. No, a scared voice answered. He might not show up.

I pushed the voice away. He had to know Natasha had taken me. He would be here. I had to remain calm.

He has no idea where I am. Yes, he will be here. *No.* Yes.

Breathe in. Breathe out.

With each breath, everything hurt. My legs. My chest. My scalp.

The ground began shaking. Vibrations ran along on the soles of my feet. Slowly, they moved up my legs, until the rhythm engulfed my entire body. Rock music coursed through my veins.

"She looks beautiful, doesn't she?"

I spun around.

"I'll say."

I turned in the other direction.

"More champagne, please."

I didn't see anyone.

"Hello?" I shouted. "Who's there?"

Oh my God. I was stuck in time, in a strange place, hearing voices.

"Hello?" I called out again.

The bass explosion inside my head was deafening. I covered my ears to quiet the sound. It was no use. It was only getting louder.

A hot breeze blew against my back, pushing me forward. When I put my foot down in front of me, it slipped, and I fell sideways onto the ground. I pushed myself to a sitting position. Something that should have been easy was now almost impossible. Even breathing took too much energy.

"Renn," I whispered. "I need you. So much, I need you." My words squeezed out between my fear.

I sat with my hands wrapped around my knees, rocking back and forth. *Please find me.*

The familiar smell was faint at first. And then it nearly swept me off the ground. This time it wasn't Renn. It was someone even better.

"Mom?" I whispered.

Her sweet cucumber scent filled the air. And just like that, I was six years old again. A calmness settled over me at the idea of my mom being present.

I rose easily to my feet. Every nerve in my body reacted to the nearness of my mom. As if being pulled by a rope, I walked forward. One foot after the other.

The sand gave way to a crowded patio with a dance floor in the center. The beach lay beyond in the distance. A band played *I Wanna Dance with Somebody Who Loves Me.* A song made famous by Whitney Houston, and one I'd heard my mother sing a million times. A song I'd heard her talk about from the best party of her life. Her wedding day.

Small gasps of air escaped from my mouth. Colored lights filled my vision.

"Mom," I whispered again.

There she was, twirling around the dance floor with my father. Her silky hair fell in waves, resting on her bare shoulders. Her gown clung to her body, showing off her tiny waist and delicate ankles.

Seeing the pearl around her neck, I instinctively touched my bare skin. I watched her rub her finger over the soft surface, remembering how I used to touch the pearl that same way before I lost it in the sand. If she gave it to me again, I would wear it for the rest of my life.

Mom whispered something in my father's ear, making him smile. Then he cupped her face in his hands and kissed her.

For a split second, I forgot I had time traveled. I was a guest at their wedding, and life would continue from this moment forward. But who would I be to them?

"They make a lovely couple," a man next to me said. He wore a beige vest and white shirt. His hair tickled the top of his shirt collar. "They're going to have beautiful children."

"Thank you," I whispered.

When the song stopped, my mom walked up to Aunt Beth and my grandmother. Mom took off her heels and tossed them under a table. She touched the shoulder of Aunt Beth's gauzy blue dress and then kissed Grandma on the cheek.

I held my cupped hands under my chin. They were the most beautiful women in the world. My family. My entire family.

My grandmother looked regal in a long, green dress. Her hair was short, like today, but instead of white, it was brown with flecks of blonde. Aunt Beth's beauty couldn't be denied. Her thick hair was pulled off to one side, held in place with a large, sparkling clip.

But my mom was the star. The stunning, shining star of the evening. And she was alive.

As I stared, something shimmered in my peripheral vision. Renn stood across the room next to a large flowerpot. He tilted his head at me.

Relief flooded through my body like a dam

exploding. He was here. He found me. But I wasn't ready to leave, not yet. I yearned to hug my mother, hold her in my arms, ask her to please not get in the car that night.

Taking a step forward, I felt a tap on my arm. "Want to dance?"

"Huh? Oh, no. Excuse me," I said, glancing at the man next to me.

It was a quick look but long enough for everything to change. When I brought my eyes back in Renn's direction, he was gone. I ran across the dance floor toward my mom.

"You stupid girl." I heard Natasha's evil laugh. And then the pain seared through my body.

This time, when the spinning ceased, I knew exactly where I was. At home in our living room. It was July 14, 1998. Six thirty-two in the evening.

The TV blared *Home Improvement* loudly into the room. My dad sat in his recliner, snoring. Our dinner simmered in the Crock-Pot.

And in exactly thirteen minutes, the phone was going to ring with the news that changed my life forever.

But not this time. I was going to change that future.

Without a second thought, I ran from our house and down the block to the intersection where the horrible man didn't stop. Where he had crashed into my mother's car, sending it spinning into a tree, taking my mom away from me forever.

I reached the corner, panting and gasping for air.

I planted myself in the middle of the street. If he saw me, he would have to stop. They said he'd been drinking and didn't see the sign. But he'd have to see a girl standing in the middle of the road.

When I heard his car zooming toward me. I jumped up and down, waving my arms and screaming until my throat hurt.

My mom's car came from my right. Her headlights lit up the street. Now for sure, he'd see me. But he wasn't stopping. And I wasn't moving out of the way.

Faster and faster, his car approached, swerving along the road.

"Stop," I screamed.

Out of nowhere, arms grabbed me and shoved me to the sidewalk. A mass of curly hair blocked my view of the accident.

But I heard it all, every shattering of glass, every crackling of the tree branches, every whir of my mom's car as it flew above me. Everything. Until the only sound left was a small girl's cry.

I struggled to get out of Arlianna's arms, to save the girl, until I realized it was me. I was sobbing. I was alive. And nothing had changed.

I couldn't stop Mom's death. Not then. Not now.

Fear paralyzed whatever strength I had left. I wanted to run over to my mom, but I couldn't move. Even as the large piece of glass dropped from the tree. Arlianna gave me a push. I felt the pain rip through my body.

And then the whiteness.

****

"Jessie!" Strong arms lifted me off the pavement and yanked me to my feet. I was back at The Getty.

"Kyle?" The color was gone from his face, leaving his eyes large and dark.

"What happened to you? Where did you go?"

213

"OhmyGod." I threw my arms around him. My whole body shook as I gasped for air. The zings shot through my body, but I didn't flinch. His arms provided me the safety I needed. "She took me. Just like she said she would. And I saw my mom and… You saw Natasha this time, didn't you?"

"No. I didn't see anything. I turned around, and you were gone. You were right there." He pointed to a spot several feet away on the grass. "And then you were here, on this path." He ran his hand up and down my back.

"I'm so cold, and I can't stop shaking. Please, don't let go of me."

He stroked my hair, holding me close. His heart hammered against my chest.

I nodded. "It was so horrible, Kyle. I saw my mom, right before she died, and I couldn't save her. I couldn't stop her. I couldn't do anything, but just watch." Tears ran down my cheeks.

"I got you." Kyle hugged me closer.

"And the sound. It's inside my head. I can't even…" I covered my ears with the palms of my hands.

"You're safe now."

"I'm back. That doesn't mean I'm safe," I said.

"You could have been hallucinating." He cupped my hands inside his.

"You said I disappeared?"

"Not exactly."

"I saw you disappear," Heather said. Her voice was barely audible. "Wha…wha…what's happening to you? Should we call 911?"

"No." I gave her a weak smile. "But thanks."

"How did you…?"

214

"Not now," Kyle interrupted. "I better get her home."

"Yeah. Um, call me later." She rubbed the side of her head. "I..I better go. I, um. It's not me, though, right? I'm not seeing things. You did…"

"It's not you, Heather."

"Let me know if you need anything. " She touched my arm, lightly, and hurried away.

Kyle held me tightly to his side as we left the garden. Without asking, he led me to the coffee kiosk in the courtyard and bought two hot lattes. It felt luscious going down, thawing my bones, and spreading throughout my body.

"She was so beautiful that day, my mother." I leaned against Kyle's shoulder, holding the take-out cup between my hands.

He didn't say anything, just kept rubbing my arm in a comforting rhythmic manner as the wedding played over and over in my mind. Renn had been at the wedding. Why hadn't he rescued me at the accident instead of Arlianna? I feared the worst.

"I couldn't save her," I whimpered.

"We can't change the past." Kyle wiped the tears off my face. "If that were possible, just think how messy things would get."

I closed my eyes, trying to block out the accident. Before, all I had was memories of the phone and my father rushing around in a panic. Now I had all those horrible crashing sounds branded inside my brain.

"She sent me there for a reason," I said. "I think she's trying to kill me."

"If it happened at all."

I tilted my head up, staring into his eyes. "Don't

think, don't analyze. Put all that aside and just go with what I'm saying. She took me, and she'll get me again."

"Not when I'm around."

Chapter Thirty-Two

Natasha pulled off her boots and tossed them across the bedroom.

Her side of the bed was in shambles. Her husband's side remained untouched. How many days had Seth been sleeping in the den? Natasha had stopped counting.

Soon. Soon it would all be over. Arlianna was gone, hopefully for good. What a fool, trying to save Jessica.

Good riddance to you, Arlianna. My once trusted friend.

It could take her years to find her way back to this time. No locator. Injured. God only knew where she'd traveled. Renn couldn't help her now. He could barely help himself. Pining away after that girl.

By this time tomorrow, she'd be rid of him too. Without Arlianna, she could now send Jessica anywhere she wanted. That little blip was sure to follow.

From her nightstand, Natasha picked up the bottle of scotch and poured herself a large glass. After taking a swallow, she turned off the holocom. The last thing she wanted to do now was receive work messages.

She set the holo-mote to The Gardens. The expansive lawn lined with every color imaginable filled her with peace. Happiness, well, that would come later.

Powerful women weren't given the luxury of knowing joy.

The door opened behind her.

"Seth? Is that you?" Finally, he'd come back to her bed. She'd apologize for taking off so suddenly the past few days. Explain to him about the problems at work. With them now in the past, she could focus solely on him. "I'm so glad you came home."

"You are?"

Natasha spun around. Renn, or his image, stood before her, with a big shit-eating grin on his face. His trench coat seemed sturdier than ever.

"That's not funny," she said, sure it was a holo. But hadn't she turned off all communication? The holo moved forward. "You've done your trick. You can vanish now." She waved her arm at the image.

Renn took another step toward her. The shimmers from his coat, waxing and waning as he got closer.

"You're not..." Natasha swallowed.

"No. It's me. In the flesh." He grinned at her.

Natasha stumbled backward. "Get out of here. Now."

"I intend to. But not before I see you arrested."

"For what?" Natasha asked. Her pulse quickened.

"For tampering with my portal."

"What in God's name are you talking about?"

"This, ma'am." A police officer clad in silver appeared behind Renn. He held out a small piece of Renn's coat.

"I never touched his coat," Natasha said. She clenched her jaw, anger spewing inside her.

"You'll have your day in court to plead your case," Renn spit out.

The officer marched forward, moving his arms robotically at his sides.

"Get out of my house. I'll have you arrested." She reached for her holocom.

She was too late. The officer pressed his belt, and the protective bubble surrounded Natasha.

"You can't do this to me. I didn't have anything to do with that ripped piece." She pounded on the invisible enclosure. "Let me out of here."

Renn's snarky smile flashed before her. He poured himself a tall glass of scotch and raised it in her direction seconds before the transport lifted into the air, carrying her away.

****

Renn stretched out on his bed, imagining Jessica by his side. He stared out his skylight at the night. His hand instinctively picked up the holo-mote to alter the view, but after spending time in the past, he wanted only to stare at reality. Stars salted the sky forming constellations he couldn't name.

He hadn't told any of his friends he was home. Tweetlyn would want to help, but he didn't want to involve her with his problems. When it was all over, he'd contact them all. Maybe they could party like they had in the past. That is, if everything went his way. But his way was going to be an uphill climb.

Renn knew it was going to take more than a piece of fabric to convict Natasha. He had to gather evidence of her tampering with Central Match and bring in witnesses. Those living happily-ever-after would be hard pressed to leave their homes and testify.

As for Arlianna, he suspected she was orbiting, trying to get home.

He had sent a dozen communications in response to her last one. It had been a cryptic message: *stem cut.* The image of her flower tattoo had been haunting him all day.

His mentor was a strong lady, but he feared she had been injured.

He picked up his cell phone. Jessica had said it was one of the smartest on the market, but it wasn't smart enough to contact her. No, he would have to make another trip in person.

He turned on the sound wall to the Whitney Houston channel. As the songs played, he drifted off to sleep imagining Jessica in a long white dress similar to one her mother wore at the beach wedding.

Hand in hand they would dance until their feet hurt, without a worry in world.

Chapter Thirty-Three

"You're jumpier than a flea-bitten filly," Pa said, wrapping his arm around me as we walked to The Mud Hut. It was only eight in the morning, but I could tell it was going to be a hot day. Either that, or I was sweating from nerves.

"That guy who killed Mom? Is there any chance of parole?" I kicked at a rock on the pavement. "He's been in jail a long time."

"Slim to nothing. He won't be getting out of the pokey anytime soon."

The image of his car speeding toward me flashed across my mind. I hoped it would lessen with time, but I knew it would never go away. "Didn't you want to kill him?" I asked.

"Darn tootin' I did. At first. But staying mad wouldn't bring your mother back. And I had you."

My father's anger may have subsided, but mine was just getting started. I kicked another rock sending it against a tree. It had been the drunk driver's third offense, but I didn't trust our judicial system.

"I thought it would get easier," I said. "But lately, I miss her more than ever."

My father stopped walking and placed his hands on my shoulders. "I miss her every day. But she's here." He placed his hand on his heart. "And she always will be."

"I know. And something else I know. Your dreams do mean something. You were mumbling weird stuff when you fell asleep in your chair last night."

"Strange, I had one last night. I haven't had one like that one in ages."

"What Renn said could be true." I looped my arm through my pa's and steered him to the left. Up ahead loomed the coffee mug shaped sign of The Mud Hut.

"I won't go down that road. But the dream sure felt real, more like a memory."

"Those are the things I want you to tell me about for my movie," I said. "So that my characters are three dimensional and believable."

"You don't need my help for that."

"Yes, I do. And I've got a title. I'm calling it *The Time Traveling Matchmaker.*"

Pa gave me a sideways glance. "Just keep it in your noggin'." He tapped my head. "Don't forget you're writing fiction."

"Most fiction is based on reality." Not wanting to get into the absurdity of time traveling with him yet again, I changed the subject. "I'm really glad Aunt Beth decided to leave. She needs to get out and have more fun."

Last night at dinner Aunt Beth announced her decision to go with Uncle Joe to Africa. After all, he was her soulmate.

"It took some conniving on my part to convince your aunt. You know how she worries about you," Pa said. "But I'll be here."

"You don't need to stay," I said, although I really wanted him to. Not to look after me, but because I knew I would miss him. "Don't get me wrong, I'm glad you're staying. But you don't have to worry about me."

"That's part of my job."

When we reached The Mud Hut, my pa opened the door for me. The coffee smells rushed forward, reminding me of my working days.

"Hey, guys," Kyle said as we approached the counter. Puffy bags showed under his eyes.

"What'd you do? Stay up all night?" I asked.

"Pretty much. I worked on my website, and I finally talked to Heather. She was pretty freaked out about what happened to you."

"Are you guys good?"

He nodded. "Friends. That's it. We sorted out a lot of things. So, what can I get you? It's on the house."

I ordered a soy latte. My father wanted a plain cup of Joe, as he put it. The fancy drink names were too much for him.

After we placed our order, Kyle motioned for me to come closer so he could whisper in my ear. "A woman came in here earlier wearing a trench coat."

A panicky sensation filled my stomach. I chewed on the side of my cheek, tasting a drop of blood on my tongue.

"She sat at that table where Renn always sat, writing on a weird shaped tablet, like he used to."

"Who was she watching?"

"Me," Kyle said.

I reached my hand across the counter, giving his hand a quick pat. "They don't want you. It's me they want."

"I'm not so sure," Kyle said. "She was watching me and tapping her fingernail on her screen. She was so intense."

"I wouldn't worry. She's probably camming, as Renn calls it, everyone who knows me. Thanks for the drinks." I moved aside to let the young couple behind me place their order.

After getting our drinks, Pa and I took a seat in the center of the coffee shop. As it was after nine, the usual morning regulars had come and gone, and now the place was filled with the all-dayers, the ones working on the next big screenplay or novel and a few moms with little kids.

My father took off his cowboy hat and hung it on the back of the empty chair next to him. "So, this is where you earn your dinero"

"It's a fun place," I said. "I'm anxious to get back on the schedule."

"You don't need to worry your pretty head about that, Jess. Just concentrate on school, like we talked about."

"We'll see." I took a sip of my drink, the first jolt of caffeine spreading throughout my body.

For the next few minutes, we sat without talking. Pa was like that. Talkative one minute. Quiet the next. Film ideas floated through my mind. I jotted them on a napkin.

"Writing?" my father asked.

I finished a thought and looked up. "I'm really glad you're here," I said.

"Ditto." He raised his take-out cup, his eyes sparking below his bushy brows.

I giggled.

My pa started to say something else but then his gaze drifted over my shoulder. Noticing the question seep into his brows, I turned around to see who stood behind me.

"Hi, Jessica." It was a young woman in a trench coat. Her voice was as soft and melodious as Arlianna's. A small tattoo of a bird covered the side of her face. When its wings fluttered, I knew immediately she was a Time Traveling Matchmaker. My stomach felt queasy.

"Is it Renn?" I started to get up. "Is he..."

"He's alive." The woman smiled. Her teeth sparkled white against her tanned skin. "Hello, Mr. Singleton. My name is Moira." She extended her hand toward my father. "It's a pleasure. I've read a lot about you."

I glanced at my father, wondering if he was going to say something to her about how preposterous Renn's story was, but instead he said, "Pleasure's mine, Ma'am."

As they shook hands, Moira's locator beeped. When she raised her arm, her trench coat crinkled, in the same manner as Renn's.

"He'll be back soon," Moira said, as if reading my mind. "It's all over." The wings on her tattoo fluttered.

"What about Arlianna?" I asked.

"MIA. For now."

I cringed, remembering the last time I saw her as the chunk of glass dropped on us. We'd made eye contact for a split second, fear vibrating between us. I prayed she was safe.

Moira glanced at her locator. "I must run. Peace." She made the peace sign, turned around, and walked out the door.

When no after-image appeared, I turned back to my father. He raised his eyebrows.

"Whoever these people are, they sure possess imaginations. I'll give you that," he said.

"Can't you admit it might all be true?" I asked.

He took a sip of his coffee. "You're stubborn just like your mom. Listening to you reminds me of her. Makes me miss her even more."

We fell back into our silence. I ran my finger over the top of my cup, remembering their wedding. I didn't think I was anywhere near as beautiful as my mom. Natasha could torture me all she wanted, but she could never take away the memory of my mother.

A few minutes later a stranger about my age dressed in bell-bottom jeans and an Indian print shirt with a matching headband walked into The Mud Hut.

Kyle had written a research paper on the Hippie Generation back in high school, and this girl looked like she stepped from one of his photographs. Her long blonde hair fell to the middle of her back. Beaded earrings dangled from her ears. The words FLOWER POWER were embroidered on her cloth purse.

But what I noticed most were her eyes. They were a dark blue with flecks of gold. As she stood in front of Kyle, his face lit up. He couldn't take his eyes off the girl's, and I knew it wasn't because of their color.

"Papa." I touched his hand. "See that girl?"

He nodded.

"I think she's Kyle's soulmate. That Moira, who was here earlier, is the matchmaker."

My father squinted as he watched them. He shook his head but didn't say anything.

During his break, Kyle sat with us. All he could talk about was the hippie. Her name was Zoe, and he said looking at her made him crazy with desire.

"She said she'd be back tomorrow." Kyle drummed his fingers on the table. "Do you think she will be?"

"Definitely," I said.

"This is so freaking weird." Kyle cracked his knuckles. "All those things you told me about Renn. I get it now."

My father closed his eyes and rocked back and forth, almost like he was in a trance. "Papa?"

He stared at me, but I knew he was remembering my mother's face.

"Are you okay?"

"Just thinking."

Perhaps he was beginning to believe he came from the past.

Kyle touched my arm. I welcomed the familiar zing. "Did she say anything about Renn?"

"He's still alive." A lump formed in my throat.

"Patience," he said.

That's what everyone kept saying. And that's what my heart was telling me, too. I just wanted Renn to get back here already so we could start our Happily Ever After.

Chapter Thirty-Four

"Why so glum?" my grandmother asked at dinner.

"It's that fella, isn't it?" Grandpa asked. "He has a friendly smile."

"He seems nice," my grandmother added. "Are you dating him?"

My face grew hot. I pushed my carrots against the last few bites of chicken on my plate.

It was impossible to lie to my grandmother. But no way I could I tell her he was a time traveler.

"He's out of town on business right now. I don't know when he's coming back."

"What's meant to be will be," Grandma said. "And you know Kyle has always been a favorite of mine."

"Grandma, we're just friends."

"Your grandmother's right." My father spooned another helping of carrots onto his plate. "And I think what's up next in your life is you go whole hog into your studies. Did you get your letter off to your advisor?"

"I sent it this afternoon."

"My gut is telling me this is going to hit the big screen by the time you're through," Pa said.

I laughed. "It's just a small project for film class."

"Don't downplay yourself." He set his fork on his plate and leaned back in his chair. "Someday you could be up for one of those Academy Award statues."

"Well, then when I'm accepting it, I'll have to thank all of you," I said, feeling extremely lucky to have this family.

The meal dragged on longer than usual. Or at least that's how I felt. After talking about my film project, we moved on to my car situation and then ended up discussing the high price of gas which led back to the days when my grandparents met and how much everything had changed since then.

After dinner, I sat with them for a while in the den, watching TV. My grandparents fell asleep, and my father and I talked for a bit. I could tell he was getting tired, and I was tired of talking around the elephant in the room. I knew if I brought up Renn, my father would spout off again and I wasn't in the mood.

Around ten, he claimed he needed to scoot off to bed.

"He's not lying," I said after kissing him on the cheek. "You'll see."

"Good night, little lady. Get a good night's sleep. Everything looks different when the sun is up."

The only difference I wanted was for Renn to be with me.

I curled under my blanket, surrounded by my thoughts, expecting a long, sleepless night. It turned out to be sleepless, but for better reasons than tossing and turning.

I was lying flat on my back, staring at the ceiling, when the scent of lemon wafted toward me. My heart sped into hyperdrive. I sat up, expecting to see Renn.

He wasn't in my apartment. But he was nearby unless Natasha was playing games again. I sat perfectly still, knowing I couldn't run from her.

After a few tortuous moments, I heard a faint knock. I walked slowly to my door, as the smell of citrus grew stronger.

"Who's there?" I called.

"It's me."

I was in Renn's arms before my mind could catch up with my actions.

He touched his lips to mine, and we kissed, like a circle with no ending. I was hardly satiated when he pulled away and smiled at me. "Jessica." His voice melted into my skin. And then we were kissing again.

The next time, I pulled away. I needed to look into his face, to know that he was really here.

"How did it go?" I ran my hand across his cheek. His short beard prickled my fingers.

"Let's not talk about that now," Renn said, pulling me against his chest. The crinkling of his trench coat felt like home. This is where I wanted to stay for the rest of my life.

"Shall we go inside?" he asked.

"Do you want something to eat? Are you hungry? Thirsty?" I pulled him toward my small fridge.

"Not for anything from your kitchen." Renn took my hand and led me to my bed. Carefully, he took off his coat and draped it on my chair. A fine, blue mist rose into the air.

He put his hands on my hips and pulled me toward him.

I couldn't control the way my body reacted. I pushed him down on the bed and climbed on top of him. As he tangled his fingers through my hair, we kissed like the world was coming to an end.

I practically tore his shirt off his body as he pulled

my T-shirt over my head. My breasts ached for his touch. All he had to do was look at me and my nipples hardened. When he cupped them in his hands, my groin pulsated.

I yanked off my sweats, tossing them to the floor. Then I pulled down his pants and pressed my body against his.

Hot skin against hot skin.

Once he was inside me, I gripped his back, squeezing every part of him. We fell into a slow rhythm. Until neither of us could stand it any longer. Our thrusting became quicker and harder, reaching that wonderful peak of release. Spent, we collapsed simultaneously, as one. Never, ever in my life had love making been like this.

"I missed you," Renn said when we lay cuddling in each other's arms.

"Ditto." My fingers danced along his chest.

I smiled, closing my eyes. I didn't want to fall asleep, but I was so happy. So relieved. My body couldn't stay awake any longer.

The next thing I knew the sun filled my apartment. When I turned to face Renn, he was staring at me.

He leaned over and kissed me lightly on the lips. "Good morning."

"Morning." I could definitely get used to this.

We lay face to face for a few minutes. My mind conjured up a future scenario. We lived in a small apartment with a cute kitchen nook. I saw us acting like a normal couple. Eating breakfast together, discussing the news. Driving over the canyon to the beach. Watching movies. Buying groceries. Bickering over silly things such as who didn't put the top back on the toothpaste. I saw us together forever. So beautiful, it was scary.

Renn pulled me even closer. Staring into my eyes, he traced the edge of my nose. Slowly, he moved his finger to my lips and down to my chin. Still staring he smiled with his lips closed.

"What?" I asked, afraid of the answer.

He didn't say anything. He didn't need to. I saw it in his eyes, darker than usual, rimmed with sadness.

"What?" I pressed.

"Jessica, I can't stay, not yet."

All those future memories knotted into a ball inside my stomach. The pressure climbed into my chest, past my throat, settling behind my eyes. The tears were only seconds from pouring out.

Renn moved his finger up my cheekbone. "There's going to be a trial against Natasha. What she did, sending me here to take you to someone else who is not your soulmate, that's grounds for a jail sentence. What she has currently, house arrest, is too lenient a punishment."

I untangled myself from Renn's body and sat up.

"But she won't be found guilty without me there to testify." He picked his clothes off the floor.

I imprinted the image of his naked body, taut with muscles, into my mind, as I watched him dress. "What about Arlianna?" I asked, remembering her curly hair brushing across my face. "She'll testify, won't she?"

"We still don't know where she is." Sadness filled the space between his words. "But she's strong. She'll be safe."

"I hope so." I hugged a pillow to my chest.

"There is some good news," he said. "I found

someone for Kyle. I made the calculations myself and Moira did the leg work. Zoe is perfect for him."

"I told you he'd help me."

"Thank him for me, will you?"

"Can't you…" I stopped talking when Renn picked up his trench coat.

Time stood still. He looked at his coat for a few seconds before putting it on. My heart slivered into tiny pieces.

He was leaving. Again. Just like that. And there was nothing I could do to stop him.

"You're going now?"

"Jessica." His eyes dazzled with his smile. "Why don't you come with me?"

"Seriously?" I clutched my hands to my chest, my smile so stretched, I thought my skin would crack. "Is that possible?"

"What Natasha did was illegal." Renn shoved his hands into the pockets of his trench coat. "But technically you're not the subject of my mission any longer. Arlianna once took someone to their future as a favor. I think we can do that now."

"And we can get back here?" I got out of bed and dressed quickly.

"Haven't I been coming back?" He placed his hands around my waist. "We can come back anytime."

Knowing my family would be worried to death if they didn't hear from me for a few days, I told them Renn and I were going camping. I threw a few pairs of jeans, T-shirts, a toothbrush, and some makeup into an overnight bag. And tossed in my cell phone. God knew why. But I took it everywhere with me. So, why not take it to the future?

"Ready?" Renn asked.

My pulse raced as I took Renn's hand. "What's it like there?" I asked.

"You'll see in a few minutes."

He placed his arm against mine, making sure the fabric was pushed tight against my skin. My breathing came in short gasps, and my pulse raced faster than I thought possible. I tried to calm it, but my heart thudded and pounded so loudly, I was sure Grandma could hear it on the other side of the door.

Renn kissed me. Something electrical passed between us, but nothing else happened. We were still in the middle of my apartment.

"Let's use both arms," Renn suggested. I nodded and swung my bag over my shoulder.

He put my hands together between both his arms and pressed. A few sparks shot into the air. Still nothing else happened.

"What's wrong?" I asked.

"Here, come inside my trench coat."

We pressed against each other. Leg against leg. Foot to foot. My head nuzzled into his chest. His heart raced faster than mine.

I closed my eyes. I wished for myself to be in the future with Renn. I felt myself rising. Moving in a circle. I clutched onto him. Inhaling his scent. I squeezed my eyes even tighter. Colors flashed against my eyelids.

And then…I heard my grandparents' landline ringing on the other side of the connecting door.

I felt totally deflated. We weren't going anyway. At least, I wasn't.

"I don't understand," Renn said. "Something isn't

working properly."

He began pacing across my small apartment.

"Our training film explained the motions." He stopped in front of me and placed a hand on each of my shoulders. "But something is off."

"Are you sure we're doing it right?"

"Positive. I studied that scene a dozen times."

"Scene?"

"From that movie I told you about. The one that inspired our business."

In that moment, it hit me like a tidal wave.

"Who wrote that movie?"

"J. Arezzo." The way he said the name was even more romantic than the picture of the town. "Why do you ask?"

"Ohmygod." I slapped my chest. Now I was the one pacing. I grabbed at the air, hoping to find a word to describe what I felt.

"What?" Renn said, stopping me from moving. "What is it?"

"Look." I showed him the postcard of the romantic town where my parents met. "I know what's wrong, Renn."

And before he could tell me that I was crazy, I told him about the movie I now knew I was destined to write. Up until that moment, I hadn't realized I would be using a pen name. But it made perfect sense.

Singleton wasn't a very romantic name, and this movie was all about romance and true love.

"I can't go with you until I finish my screenplay," I explained. "It's the movie you're talking about. I've been going in circles trying to get it right. And now I know what I need to do."

"Damn." Renn stared at me. "You're even more beautiful when you get passionate. But this is…"

"The truth."

"You're J. Arezzo?" Renn shook his head. "Incredible."

Renn sank to the floor with his back against my bed.

I sat down next to him, leaning my head on his shoulder. "If you tell me how it ends it will help me write faster."

"I can't tell you that. Law #29."

"You can stay here while I work on it," I suggested, knowing that I was asking the impossible.

"You know I can't do that."

"But what if…"

He traced his finger along my lips. "Don't say a word. I will be back."

"When?"

"When you finish the movie. Like you said."

"But you've been going back and forth," I reminded him.

He cupped my head in his hands, running his thumbs along my hairline. He took long, deep breaths, studying every part of me, everything. "We can't chance it anymore. Now that we know. Too many things could change."

When I looked into his eyes, I saw the unshed tears. He pressed his lips on mine, kissing me deeply yet with a tenderness I knew I would carry with me forever.

"I love you," I whispered.

"I know. I love you, too."

And then he was gone. Just like that. All that was

left was his lemony scent, lingering in the spot where he stood seconds ago. And would hopefully be standing again someday.

Outside, I heard my tree brush up against the window. I picked up the leaves Renn had given me, sat down at my computer, and opened a new file.

The Time Traveling Matchmaker
By J. Arezzo

I didn't know everything that was going to happen in my screenplay, but I knew that eventually my lovers were going to find their *after*. That Renn and I would be together again someday.

"I love you, Renn," I whispered.

I wiped away my tears and began typing as fast as possible.

****

Mission Statement – The Time Traveling Matchmaker's Handbook

There is one and only one true soulmate for each of us born into this world. Those lucky enough to have been born into the same time have the chance to meet and love and live as one. As a consequence, those who are not born into the same time shall depend on Time Traveling Matchmakers, Inc. We must never falter in our obligations. We at Time Traveling Matchmakers, Inc. are committed to using the technology provided us, to bring soulmates together, to live as one, in harmony, peace, and LOVE.

Once upon a time in the distant future there lived…

Epilogue

One year later ~*~ "Congratulations, Mrs. Porter."
Kyle clinked his champagne flute against mine.

I took a slow sip, savoring the robust flavor. I
wanted to remember every single moment of this day.
From waking up as the sun lightened my bedroom, to
slipping my feet into Lilly's red heels and then down
the aisle with my arm looped through my father's.

I wanted to forget last year. My desire for Renn
had powered me through hour upon hour at my
computer, writing as fast as possible.

Once finished, I had been relentless in getting my
screenplay in the hands of the right people.

Now, one year to the day since Renn and I had
attempted our time travel, my screenplay, *The Time
Traveling Matchmaker*, was in production at a major
studio.

And I was a bride.

After a grueling six-month trial, Natasha had been
convicted and was serving three consecutive life
sentences. Renn assured me she would never get out on
parole.

As for Arlianna, Renn was hopeful. He had
received a cryptic message from her a few weeks ago.

From across the reception hall, a burst of laughter
caught my attention. Renn and my father stood
together, both with a cherry pop tucked in the corner of

their mouth.

I still couldn't get over seeing Renn without his trench coat. Today, he looked exceptionally handsome in the light grey tux Kyle had helped him buy. It hugged his body in all the right places. A pleasurable warmth spread through me as I imagined undressing him later this evening.

"I'm sorry I ever doubted you." Kyle nodded in Renn's direction. "Look at us. Married people. Who would have thought?

"Where is your Mrs. Time Traveler?" I asked.

"Mingling," Kyle said. "Zoe loves to talk."

"She's fitting in then?"

Kyle nodded. "More than I expected. She doesn't remember anything. Just like your father, she has these recurring dreams. Hers are about protesting the Vietnam war, and she wakes up disoriented and sad. And don't get me started on technology."

"But you're happy?"

Kyle beamed at me. "More than ever. Ah, here he is."

Renn joined us, putting his arm around me. "Hello, my beautiful bride."

I leaned into his chest, inhaling that lemon scent I'd come to love, feeling the tingles work their way through my body to my groin. It was all I could do to contain myself.

"Congratulations, my man." Kyle slapped Renn on the back. "I wish the two of you all the happiness this time has to offer."

"How was Hawaii?" Renn asked.

"Amazing. Fancy drinks with little umbrellas. Sun. Surf. Where are you guys going on your honeymoon?"

Kyle asked.

"That's up to my wife." Renn turned to me.

Wife. It still didn't seem real.

"Can we go anywhere in time?" I asked

"Do you have someplace special in mind?"

"Maybe"

Right now, I was happy to be where I was. The room radiated with lightness. My grandmother sat talking to Uncle Joe. Her hands sliced through the air with their conversation. Aunt Beth danced with my grandfather. She caught my eye and smiled. At a table, Lilly chatted with Nola and Ashley. My mind slipped my mom into each frame. "*I wanna dance with somebody.*" Whitney Houston's voice filled the hall.

"May I have this dance?" Pa extended his hand. "Do you mind?" he asked Renn.

"No, sir," Renn said.

I took my father's hand as he led me onto the dance floor. He spun me into a twirl and then pulled me close to his chest.

"You know, little lady," Pa said. "Your wedding reminds me of the day I married your mother."

"Me, too."

As we danced, images of my parents' wedding played through my mind. The beach setting. The stars. The salty air. My mother's radiance. Maybe I was a lot like mother.

"I'm going to miss you," I said.

"I won't be gone that long." Pa kissed the top of my head. "I'll do my takes, wrap it up, and I'll be home by Thanksgiving. I promise."

"You don't have to promise," I said.

"I know. But I want to. Do me one favor."

"Anything."

"I know you are going somewhere special for your honeymoon, and for some reason I think I know why," my dad spoke in a wistful tone.

"If it's possible." I couldn't see the expression on his face, but I felt his arms tighten around my back.

"When you get there..." Pa leaned closer. With the scent of cherry on his breath, he whispered in my ear. "Tell your mother I'll always love her."

A word about the author…

Janie Emaus believes when the world is falling apart, we're just one laugh away from putting it together again. Her stories, essays, and poems have been published in numerous magazines, on websites, and in anthologies. In 2016, she won honorary mention in the Erma Bombeck Writing Competition. To learn more about Janie, visit her website at janieemaus.com.

Thank you for purchasing
this publication of The Wild Rose Press, Inc.

For questions or more information
contact us at
info@thewildrosepress.com.

The Wild Rose Press, Inc.
www.thewildrosepress.com